Driving A Hard Bargain . . .

A man entered the office of a car rental agency and began to tell the clerk behind the desk a story about a terrible driver.

"We very nearly had an accident, and I'd really like to give him a piece of my mind. I'd just like to find out who the guy is and where I can find him," he said pressing a crisp twenty-dollar bill into the clerk's hand.

The man recited the license number of the car. The clerk looked it up and gave him the man's name—Remo Randisi.

The man left the rental agency and crossed the street to a large black car. He got in the back, where another man was waiting for him, and repeated the information he'd gotten from the clerk.

"Very good," the other man said. "Now we'll handle this Remo, whoever he is."

"Do you think he's a cop?" the first man asked.

"If he is," the second man said, "he's a dead one."

Other books in THE DESTROYER series from Pinnacle Books

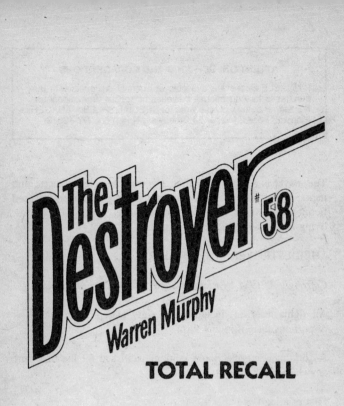

The Destroyer #58

Warren Murphy

TOTAL RECALL

PINNACLE BOOKS   NEW YORK

THE DESTROYER #58: TOTAL RECALL

Copyright © 1984 by Richard Sapir and Warren Murphy

An original Pinnacle Books edition, published for the first time anywhere.

First printing/December 1984

ISBN: 0-523-41568-0

Can. ISBN: 0-523-43103-1

Cover art by Gil Cohen

Printed in the United States of America

PINNACLE BOOKS, INC.
1430 Broadway
New York, New York 10018

9 8 7 6 5 4 3 2 1

TOTAL
RECALL

CHAPTER ONE

Billy Martin was fifteen years old, and already he was a repulsive little toad. That meant that when he grew up, he might graduate to a full-fledged snake—if he grew up.

Which right now looked doubtful because Billy Martin was in jail, charged with the murder of his parents, whom he had bludgeoned to death while they slept in their home in the Detroit suburbs.

The judge who handled the youth's arraignment was Wallace Turner, a notorious bleeding heart who could somehow find, in his speeches, some reason to blame society for every crime committed against it. The press covering the arraignment winked at each other, knowing that Billy would not only be released without bail; he might very well get a medal from Judge Turner for not killing his parents earlier. After all, it must have been their fault that their son was a murderer. But Turner surprised everyone. He ordered

1

Billy held for trial as an adult murderer and set a half-million-dollar bail. He would stay in jail, Turner said. He belonged in jail.

Turner's harsh action shocked everyone involved with the Billy Martin case—everyone except the prosecutor, who had told the judge before the proceedings that if the Martin kid were set free like every other juvenile killer who went before Turner, the prosecutor would be sure to let the press in on Turner's relationship with a woman in Grosse Pointe who went by the professional name of Didi the Dominatrix.

"You can posture and preach from the bench all you want, Wally," the prosecutor said. "Just so you know when to bend in the wind." He winked at Judge Turner.

Turner winked back and bent so fast he almost broke his back. At the arraignment, he announced in his mellowest tones that the crime involved was of such heinous character that he would be derelict in his duty if he were lenient.

Immediately after announcing his decision, Judge Wallace Turner left the bench and retreated to his chambers, where he removed his robes and sat behind his desk with a sigh to await a phone call. Even though he was expecting it, he jumped when the phone rang.

"Judge Turner," he said into the receiver.

"Satisfactory," a man's voice said in low tones. "Very satisfactory."

"Uh, th-thank you," the judge stammered, but by the time he got it out, he was holding a dead phone.

*   *   *

Across town another phone rang, this one in the office of a lawyer named Harvey Weems. Weems had not won a case in four years, but he was without equal as an ambulance chaser. When the phone rang, he looked at it dispassionately, trying to decide whether or not to answer it. Lately, no one called him except creditors and clients threatening to sue him for mishandling their cases.

After fifteen rings, he couldn't take the suspense any longer. "Attorney's office."

"Is this Harvey Weems, the lawyer?" a man's voice asked.

"Yeah, yeah," Weems said wearily. "How much do I owe you?"

"You don't owe me anything, Mr. Weems."

"All right. How much do you want to sue me for?"

"I don't want to sue you, either."

"I don't owe you money, and you don't want to sue me?"

"That's right."

"You asked for me by name," Weems said, puzzled, "so you can't have the wrong number."

"This phone call could mean a lot of money to you," the voice said.

"Really?"

"Unless I end it now."

Not one to be slow on the uptake, Weems got the idea and shut up.

"Thank you. Mr. Weems, I have a job for you. Have you read about the Billy Martin case?"

"The kid who pounded his parents to death in their sleep? Yeah, I know a little about it."

"Very good. We—I would like you to post bail for the young man and get him out of jail."

"Post bail?" Weems asked, incredulous. "Do you know how much Judge Turner set bail for? Who in his right mind would go for that much loot to put that little pissant on the street again?"

"I would."

"Uh, you would?"

"Yes, and I'll pay you ten percent of that amount to pay the bail for me."

"Ten percent? That's very . . . generous," Weems said, writing the figure down on the piece of paper and then drawing a heart around it.

"The money will be delivered to you in one hour, in small, used bills. Included will be your fee."

"In cash?" Weems asked, writing *I.R.S.* on the piece of paper but not drawing a heart abound it. Instead he drew a happy face with the three initials forming the nose.

"In cash. Take your fee out, then take the rest and bail out Billy Martin."

"Uh, what am I supposed to do with him after I get him out?" Weems asked. "He *did* just make himself an orphan, you know."

"There will be a piece of paper in with the money, with an address on it. Give it to him, and then forget about him."

"Forget him? You mean he won't be my client?"

"You are being paid to bail him out, Mr. Weems, not to represent him. Give him the address, forget him, and forget this conversation. You are being paid quite a lot of money for this job. In cash. If I thought that you weren't obeying my instructions to the letter, I'd have to notify the I.R.S. You wouldn't want that, would you?''

"No," Weems said, drawing a larger heart around the smaller one containing the figure that represented his fee. "No, I wouldn't like it. You're the boss, Mr.—''

"The money will be in your office within the hour, Mr. Weems. There won't be any reason for us to talk again after this."

The man hung up without saying good-bye, leaving a puzzled Harvey Weems holding a dead line.

Fifty-three minutes later, there was a knock on Harvey Weems's office door, and he got up to answer it.

"Mr. Weems?" a young kid asked. He couldn't have been any older than Billy Martin, the one Weems was supposed to bail out.

"That's right, kid. Who're you?"

"I have something for you."

The kid picked up a brown attaché case he had put down alongside the wall next to the door and handed it to the lawyer.

"Is this the money?"

"That's what I was supposed to give you," the boy said, and then he left.

Screw him, Weems thought, closing the door. I wasn't going to tip him, anyway.

He carried the case to his desk and opened it up.

Neatly piled stacks of used bills, banded together, stared up at him. For a fleeting moment Weems wondered what was to stop him from taking it all and disappearing. He took out the stacks that comprised his fee and put them in his desk, then closed the case, regretting that he didn't have the courage to find out.

He picked up the case and headed across town to bail out Billy Martin. Weems knew that the little punk was probably guilty of murdering his own parents. The pissant had practically admitted it. But Harvey Weems didn't much care. He had his fee, and he was just glad that he didn't have to defend the little snot to earn it.

That was going to be somebody else's headache.

He thought.

Jail did little to dampen Billy Martin's insolence. Weems could see that on the kid's face.

"What the hell do you want?" the kid demanded.

"I'm the man who bailed you out, son," Weems said.

"So give yourself a medal, fatso," Billy said, brushing past him.

Weems was in his early forties, easily old enough to be Billy Martin's father. He found just the possibility of that disturbing.

"Well, what are you waiting for? You want maybe I should fall to my knees and thank you?" Billy sneered.

"I don't expect anything of you, kid. Come on. The paperwork is done. Let's go outside."

Weems and Billy walked outside and stopped halfway down the front steps of the building. "This is where we part company, sonny," Weems said.

"Fine with me."

"Here."

Billy took the piece of paper Weems was offering him and asked, "What's this supposed to be?"

"That's an address. I suspect it's where the man who put up the money for your bail lives. Maybe *he* expects you to thank him. 'Bye, Billy," Weems said, and walked away.

If someone had approached him at that moment and asked him a question about Billy Martin, his reply would have been, "Billy who?"

All he had in mind was the money that was locked in his desk.

Billy looked down at the address on the piece of paper; it meant nothing to him. In spite of his bravado, he was curious about the man who was willing to put up all that money to bail him out. When he had first heard about the bail, he thought he knew who it had come from, but the address he now held in his hands was not familiar.

Who could his mysterious benefactor be, then? And if he was willing to pay so much to get him out, how much more might he be willing to cough up?

Greed was the determining factor in Billy Martin's decision to check out the address. If the guy was willing to come across with some more money, Billy could use it to get out of town. He had reasons to leave Detroit, and the criminal charges hanging over his head weren't the half of it.

Billy had little money of his own, which had been returned with the rest of his things when he was released from jail. He decided to hang on to what he did have and walk to the address. He knew the part of town it was in. It wasn't more than half a mile's walk.

He walked down the remainder of the steps and started on his way, oblivious to the fact that he was being followed by three people.

The three young men who were following Billy had their drill down pat. One was immediately behind him, one was across the street, and one was walking ahead of him. The way they had it set up, he was impossible to lose. They followed him discreetly until they approached the run-down section of town where the address on the slip of paper in Billy's pocket could be found.

There was little foot traffic in this part of town. There weren't that many people brave enough—or foolish enough—to walk there. It was a measure of Billy Martin's insolence that walking in that area didn't bother him at all. After all, hadn't he just about beaten a double murder rap? Did the court actually expect him to show up on the date of his trial? He'd be long gone by then.

Actually, he *would* be long gone by then, but not in the way he was planning.

Closing in on their destination, the three young men started to close ranks on Billy. The man in front of him slowed down while the man behind him quickened his pace, and the one across the street came over to his side.

As a matter of fact, they weren't really men at all. They weren't much older than Billy himself. One of them was the same boy who had delivered the money to Weems's office.

Billy was so intent on reaching his destination that he scarcely noticed the person walking ahead of him until suddenly that person had slowed enough for Billy to overtake him. As Billy came within a few steps of passing him, the other boy stopped abruptly and turned.

"Hi, Billy," he said.

Billy recognized him and stopped short. He took a couple of backward steps, but by that time the other two had caught up, and he bumped into them.

"Hey, fellas—"

The other two each took one of Billy's arms, and following the first boy, they led him down an alley that had been specially chosen for its purpose.

"Hey, guys, come on—" Billy was stammering, his tough-guy front vanished.

The others ignored him, and as he increased his efforts to escape, his captors increased the pressure of their hold on him.

"This is far enough," the first boy said, turning. The others released Billy's arms and pushed him violently toward the back of the alley. He lost his balance and sprawled on the dirty ground, skinning his hands and knees.

Pushing himself to his feet, he watched the three boys approach him and then heard three barely audible sounds—*snik! snik! snik!*—as three sharp blades appeared in their hands as if by magic.

"Aw, guys—" he started, backing up with his hands raised in front of him.

Two of the boys stepped forward and swung their blades, and blood began to gush from each of Billy's palms as he cried out from the pain.

"Please—" he shouted, but his plea fell on three sets of deaf ears.

All three boys stepped forward now, and their blades were a blur of motion that Billy tried to follow until a veil of blood fell over his eyes, and he could no longer see. It was several moments before his ability to feel went too, and that was when the three boys stepped back and retracted their blades with the same three smacking sounds.

One boy briefly checked Billy for signs of life. Failing to find any, he nodded to his companions and led the way out of the alley.

The Billy Martin who lay on the filthy cobblestones of the alley, strips of flesh flayed from his bones, bore little resemblance to the little pissant who had clubbed his parents to death without a second thought while they slept.

Billy Martin died as he had lived—a repulsive little toad who never had a chance to ascend to the higher rank of full-fledged snake.

CHAPTER TWO

His name was Remo, and people had to be taught that only he could get away with murder.

Murder belonged in the hands of someone who could do it right, for the right reasons, and that someone was Remo. He was in the resort town of Little Ferry, Virginia, to teach this lesson to retired police chief Duncan Dinnard.

Chief Dinnard had built up a fortune at the expense of the residents and tourists of Little Ferry and had now retired to sit back and enjoy it. He had turned the small Virginia town into the kind of place where if you had enough money—and paid *him* enough of it—you could literally get away with murder.

"Don't be fooled by the fact that he's retired," Dr. Harold W. Smith had told both Remo and Chiun. "He still rules that small town with an iron hand. It's time he was retired for good."

Smith could be no plainer than that.

*   *   *

Duncan Dinnard had no fear. He was a multimillionaire, with a mansion and a yacht, both of which suited his position. In addition, his property and his person were protected by the best people and the best security devices that money could buy.

At the moment, the obese Dinnard was in his mansion, entertaining the best female companionship that money could buy. The farthest thing from his mind was his own death.

If need be, he could buy that off too.

"Very impressive setup," Remo said to the wispy-haired Oriental beside him as they examined Dinnard's defenses.

"It is not necessary to compliment a man whom one is about to assassinate," the elderly Korean said loftily. "It is considered bad form."

"Oh, I see," Remo said. "Murder's okay, but tackiness can never be forgiven."

Chiun snorted. "If that were true, you would have no friends at all. Please proceed." He waved an imperious hand at the front gates. "I wish to dispense with this trivia quickly."

"What's the matter? Afraid you'll miss one of your TV soaps?"

"The Master of Sinanju no longer wastes his time on sex-laden daytime dramas."

"Oh, no?"

"No," Chiun said. "As a matter of fact, I've just begun work on an epic poem. An Ung poem. The finest piece of Ung since the Great Master Wang."

The old Oriental swaggered as he walked. "It is about a butterfly."

"Oh," Remo said.

"I've already completed the first one hundred and sixty-five stanzas of the prologue."

"That's okay, Chiun. I'm sure it'll flesh out in the final draft."

"Insolent lout. I should have known that a white boy untrainable in the subtle arts of Sinanju would lack the refinement to appreciate beauty as well."

"I'm as refined as the next white lout," Remo said.

Chiun's complaints about Remo's shortcomings no longer bothered him. He had been hearing the same complaints for more than ten years, since the first time Remo was introduced to the old master in a gymnasium in the sanitarium where Remo found himself the morning after he died.

Actually, he never died in the first place. It would have been nice if someone—anyone—had gone to the trouble of informing Remo that he wasn't really going to die in the electric chair he was plugged into, but bygones were bygones.

During those terrible moments in the chair, Remo's life didn't flash before his eyes. The only thing that did register was the ridiculous, laughable injustice of recent events. Remo Williams had been a rookie cop with the Newark Police Department, who had been sentenced to fry in an electric chair because a drug dealer he'd been chasing had had the misfortune to die. Remo hadn't killed the pusher, but he'd been the most convenient person to blame at the time. So he'd

gone to the chair and tried not to think about anything too much, and when he woke up, he was in a
windowless hospital room in a place called Folcroft
Sanitarium in Rye, New York.

For a brief moment Remo thought he must be in
heaven, but the face peering into his own disabused
him of any otherworldly notions. It was Harold W.
Smith's face, a pinched, lemony face spanned by a
pair of steel-rimmed spectacles and a permanent scowl.
Dr. Smith was, as always, wearing a three-piece gray
suit and carrying an attaché case. He never asked
Remo how he felt about coming back from the dead.
He didn't have to. Dr. Harold W. Smith had engi-
neered everything, from the false arrest on.

Remo complained that since he was officially dead,
he had no identity. Dr. Harold W. Smith seemed
pleased. At least, he had shuffled his papers with a
little more gusto than before. It was as close as Smith
got to acting pleased.

He took Remo to the gymnasium to meet Chiun.
The eighty-year-old Oriental would, he explained,
make a new man of Remo. And he did: Remo became,
through the years, a man who could live under water
for hours at a time. Who could catch arrows in his
bare hands. Who could climb up the sheer faces of
buildings without the aid of ropes or ladders. Who
could count the legs on a caterpillar as it inched
across his finger. Who could walk with no sound and
yet hear the heartbeat of a man a hundred yards
away. For what Chiun taught him was not a technique or a trick, but the very sun source of the
martial arts.

The old Korean was the Master of Sinanju, and possibly the most dangerous man alive. Harold Smith had hired him to train a man for a mission so secret that even Chiun himself could not be told about it. The mission was to work as the enforcer arm of an organization so illegal that its discovery could well mean the end of the United States. CURE belonged to America, but America could not claim the organization because CURE worked completely outside the Constitution. CURE blackmailed. And kidnaped. And killed. Because sometimes those methods were necessary in fighting crime.

Remo Williams was trained to kill. Silently, quickly, invisibly, as only a master of Sinanju could kill. Harold W. Smith directed Remo to the targets, and Remo eliminated them.

The target this time was Duncan Dinnard, whose mansion loomed now in front of Remo and Chiun. The house was surrounded by guards, obviously armed.

"Okay, everybody up. Rise and shine," Remo shouted, clapping his hands and whistling.

"Who goes?" one of the guards called out, holding his handgun in firing position.

"White garbage," Chiun said under his breath.

"What did he say?" the guard demanded.

"He said we're here to collect the garbage," Remo answered.

"He's a garbage man?" the second guard asked, looking at Chiun suspiciously.

"Civil service," Remo said, as if that explained everything.

"He don't look like no garbage man I ever saw," the first guard said.

"Besides, we don't have any garbage left. It was picked up yesterday."

"That's where you're wrong," Remo said.

"Whadaya mean?" the first guard asked.

"You do have some garbage left."

"Like what?" the second guard asked.

"Like you," Remo said.

The bars on the gate were very close together, much too close for a human body to fit between them under ordinary circumstances.

Remo's hands sped between the bars, took hold of each man by the throat, and pulled. By the time the two men had been squeezed between the bars, they were dead, crushed to death or electrocuted, which-ever came first.

"Sloppy," Chiun said, shaking his head in disgust.

"It worked, didn't it? I'm going over." Remo opened his hands and let both men slump to the ground.

He vaulted the twelve-foot high fence from a stand-ing position, and when he landed on the other side, Chiun was standing there waiting for him.

"Between the bars," Chiun said, smirking. "Some of us are above cheap and flamboyant displays."

"Cheap—"

"Let us get this over with," the old Oriental interrupted. "I'll go to the boat. You try the house."

"First one to find Dinnard gets to do the dirty deed," Remo said.

Chiun closed his eyes and said, "One does not refer to one's profession as a 'dirty deed.' "

"Come on, Little Father. Do you think I'm a complete idiot? Wait, don't answer that."

"A wise decision," Chiun said, and headed for the dock where Chief Dinnard's yacht was moored.

Remo started for the mansion, came across ferocious guard dogs twice, reasoned with them, and left them unconscious but unhurt. There was no reason in the world to kill a dumb animal.

Remo approached the house, having passed by countless TV security cameras without being seen by one. Thinking invisible, as he had been taught to do by the Master of Sinanju, could work wonders for a body.

His next decision was whether to simply force the door and enter or ring the doorbell. He decided that it would be more interesting to ring the bell.

"Whadaya want?" the man who answered the door asked.

"Do all you fellas have the same manners?"

"What?"

"Never mind. Is Chief Dinnard in?"

"Who wants to know?"

Remo looked left, right, behind him, then back at the big man and said, "I guess I do."

"Funny man," the guy said, and started to close the door.

Remo put one finger on the door and it stopped cold. No matter how hard the other man tried to push, it wouldn't budge.

"Hey," he said, staring at Remo's finger. "How're you doing that?"

"Leverage. Is the chief at home?"

Still impressed, the man replied, "Yeah, he's home. Hey, could you teach me that?"

"What?"

"That," the man said, pointing to Remo's finger. "Leverage."

"You want to learn leverage?"

"Sure."

"Watch," Remo said. He took his finger from the door and held it up in front of the man's face, catching and holding his eyes. In one quick motion the finger flicked forward, the man's eyes rolled up into his head, and he slumped to the floor.

"Well, if you're not going to pay attention . . ." Remo said, stepping over the prone body of the sleeping man. "Don't worry, I'll find him myself."

The house was huge, but Remo's instincts were operating one hundred percent, and he felt as if he could smell Dinnard's presence in the house. He smelled something else too. Perfume. A woman— there was a woman in the house with Dinnard, which could be a complication.

Following his nose through the huge house, Remo finally came to an opulently furnished bedroom, with mirrors and pillows and a huge bed. On the bed was an equally huge man, being ministered to by a lovely blond woman with big, smooth, pink-nippled breasts, delicate hands, and a full-lipped mouth, all of which were in use at the moment.

Neither the woman nor the chief noticed Remo as he entered the room and approached the bed. She was grunting and moaning with effort, while Dinnard was grunting and moaning with pleasure.

"Excuse me, miss," Remo said, looking over the woman's bare shoulder.

"Huh?" she said, staring at him in surprise. He placed his hand on her smooth back and exerted pressure on her fifth vertebra. A blank look came over her face as she experienced more pleasure than she had ever before felt in her life. Slowly the corners of her generous mouth curved up, and then she keeled over on the bed, oblivious to what was going on around her. She would remain that way for some time.

Dinnard, who moments before had been languishing in sensations of his own, slowly became aware that the blonde had stopped working on him.

"Hey, Sally," he said, his eyes slowly beginning to focus again. "What's the matter?"

"Sally's taken the rest of the afternoon off, Dinnard," Remo said. "I'm her replacement."

"What? Who the hell are you? How'd you get in here?"

"Which question do you want answered first?"

"Who the hell are you?" Dinnard snapped, trying to push himself up into a seated position. Remo placed one hand on his chest and exerted just enough pressure to keep him on his back.

"I'm the garbage collector," he said.

"What the hell are you talking about?" Dinnard demanded, his face turning red from the effort he was expending in trying to sit up. "Do you know who I am?"

"I know, Chief," Remo said. "You're a fat piece of slime who's had this little town under his thumb long enough. I'm here to take out the garbage for good."

"What garbage?"

"You."

"You're crazy. Leo!"

"Is that the man who answers your door?"

"Leo!"

"He can't answer you. He's taking a nap."

"I've got guards at the gate."

"They're taking a permanent nap."

"I've got dogs. Did you kill them?"

"Of course not," Remo said, looking hurt. "Do I look like the kind of man who would hurt a dumb animal?"

"What do you want? You want money? I can give you a lot of money."

"You know, there was a time in my life when I might have said yes to an offer like that."

"For a split second, Remo thought back to that time, the time before Smith and CURE and Chiun, but then he shook his head and decided that he was better off now.

"I've got an awful lot of money," Dinnard said.

"I'm afraid I don't like the way you made your money, Chief."

"Look, I'll do anything you want, anything . . ."

"Be quiet, then. Take the end like a man."

"The end?" Dinnard screeched like a woman. "What do you mean the end?"

"I mean that your time has come, Duncan Dinnard. This is your death!" Remo said in his best game-show voice. At least, he hoped it was his best. He hadn't seen a game show in a long time.

"Glug—" Dinnard started to say, but he couldn't speak after that because Remo's hand had tightened on his chest, just over the heart, and suddenly the chief's heart was beating very rapidly, picking up speed until the fragile organ couldn't take it anymore and just exploded.

Remo found Chiun seated on the dock next to Dinnard's yacht, staring out at the water. "Composing some more Dung—oops—Ung poetry?" he asked.

"Do not be insolent with me."

"I'm sorry, Little Father."

"It took you all this time to accomplish our purpose here?"

"Well, I had to give some lessons in leverage, and—"

"I do not wish to hear your excuses. On top of everything else, your technique was faulty."

"You were down here and I was up there," Remo said, then asked, knowing that he was going to be sorry; "How do you know my technique was faulty?"

"I know," Chiun said cryptically. He looked at his student and sniffed once. "Also, you have the scent of a woman on you, and a white woman, at that. No doubt you were indulging in pleasures of the flesh while you were supposed to be working."

"Who, me? How can you say such a thing?"

"Because you are an ungrateful lout who has allowed the Master of Sinanju to sit out here alone, waiting, while you rutted about. . . ."

"I did not! As a matter of fact—"

He was drowned out by the din of an explosion coming from Dinnard's house.

"You took care of the yacht?" Remo asked Chiun.

"Yes, you took care of the house, I see."

"Gas line."

Chiun stood up and said, "We can go, then? Have you finished wasting my vauluable time?"

"Smith won't think it was a waste," Remo said.

"Perhaps. But I am concerned with technique, with execution, with the poetry of the movement. Your Philistine Emperor Smith is concerned only with results," he sniffed.

"I'm satisfied with the results," Dr. Harold W. Smith said, leaning back in his chair behind his desk at Folcroft Sanitarium.

"See?" Chiun said to Remo.

"Excuse me?" Smith asked. "Did I miss something?"

"He knew you were going to say that," Remo said.

"Say what?"

"That you were satisfied."

"Why shouldn't I be?" Smith asked, looking at Chiun, but it was Remo who answered.

"My technique was faulty."

"Oh," Smith said. "Er—you'd better work on that, Remo." Chiun tittered. "At any rate," Smith continued, "the assignment was relatively minor. I've got something else for you."

"Something that does not require good technique," Chiun said.

Smith ignored him. "A fifteen-year-old boy was murdered in Detroit three days ago. A William—Billy—Martin. He was stabbed to death by at least three people with knives."

Remo shook his head. "That's too bad. But it's a case for the police, not us."

"A child has been killed," Chiun said indignantly, as if that explained it all, Remo was afraid that Chiun was going to go off on one of his diatribes concerning the holiness of children, but Smith cut him off.

"Let me explain. This is just the most recent in a rash of juvenile murders around the country."

"What's the spread?"

"It's happened more often in Detroit, but we've also had reports from New York, Los Angeles, and New Orleans."

"What was this last kid's claim to fame?"

"He murdered his parents, most likely, although he was killed before his trial."

"Sweet kid."

"He beat them to death with a baseball bat or something while they were asleep."

"What was he doing on the street?"

"He was out on bail."

"What the hell kind of laws do they have in Detroit?" Remo asked.

"Everybody was surprised," Smith said, "especially considering the judge who was on the bench for the arraignment. No explanation. The kid was just out on bail."

"How long?"

"How long what?"

"How long was he out on bail before he was killed?"

"Less than an hour."

"So somebody set him up. They went his bail to get him out so they could kill him."

There was silence for a moment, then Remo asked, "What about the others? Were they killers too, or just hubcap snatchers?"

"Some of them had records, but none had been arrested for murder."

"So what do you want us to do? Find out who killed the killer? I mean, if the kid killed his own parents, who cares who killed him, anyway?"

"He was a child," Chiun said, and Remo knew it was just a matter of time now.

"Whatever," Smith said in exasperation. "Go to Detroit, since that's where the most recent incident was."

"Incident?" Chiun shrieked, and Remo knew that zero hour was finally upon them. "You call the murder of a child an incident?"

Smith looked at Remo, who shrugged and prepared for the verbal onslaught that was about to take place.

"Children are promises of greatness . . ."

"I know," Remo said.

". . . in all manners possible."

Remo gave Smith an I've-heard-it-all-before look and said, "I know, Chiun."

"They have all been made holy in our eyes."

"Chiun—"

"They are the hope of the future. . . ."

"Chiun—"

"You cannot kill hope. It is unthinkable. It is against the laws of Sinanju."

Remo gave up and said to Smith, "Do you have our tickets?"

"Yes," Smith said. "You're on a flight to Detroit tonight." He handed Remo the tickets.

"No matter what the child did, no one had the right to kill him."

"We know, Chiun, we know," Remo said, getting to his feet. "Come on, we have some packing to do."

"It is unthinkable," Chiun said, standing up. "It is our responsibility to find out who is committing this most despicable of crimes."

"I agree, Chiun," Remo said. "It's our responsibility."

"Good luck," Smith said.

"We will not need luck," Chiun assured him. "This is something that must be done, and it will be done. I so swear."

And with that Chiun strode purposefully from the room. Remo shrugged at Smith and said, "He'll walk all the way to Detroit if I don't stop him. We'll keep in touch."

CHAPTER THREE

Remo and Chiun stopped at their hotel just long enough to drop off their luggage and then proceeded immediately to a car rental agency. They did not go to the number-one company but to one of the others because Chiun always said that he had respect for anyone who was constantly trying harder.

Remo would have liked to take a few moments to breathe, but it was Chiun who pushed him to rent a car hurriedly so that they could drive over to the police station where Billy Martin had been arrested and bailed out.

"These child killers must not be allowed to roam the streets any longer than is absolutely necessary," was the way he put it.

"I know how you feel—" Remo started, but Chiun took exception to the remark and made a disgusted noise, cutting his student off.

"Of course you do not know how I feel. You have

never seen a child drowned because of famine, as I have. You have never known the sorrow of Sinanju—"

"All right, Chiun," Remo said, "all right." He'd been forced to listen to Chiun's pontification on the same subject on the plane all the way to Detroit. "You're right, I don't know how you feel, I admit it, but I just can't seem to get all worked up over the murder of some little snot who killed his own parents."

Chiun gave Remo a withering stare and said, "I cannot find the proper words to describe how I feel toward you at this moment."

"I'm sure you'll come up with something."

"To think that I have struggled all these years to impart to you the knowledge of a master of Sinanju, and you cannot even respond to the murder of a child."

"Listen, Chiun," Remo said from behind the wheel of the car, "I cried when Old Yeller died, really I did—"

"Old who?"

"It was a dog in a movie I saw when I was a kid—"

"You liken the death of a child to the death of a . . . an animal? A dog?"

Remo decided that he had better keep his mouth shut because when he did open it, he was just making things worse.

He continued to drive, trying to block out the sound of Chiun's recriminations, a tall order, even for him. The old Oriental had not run out of them by the time they reached the police station, but he apparently decided to save what he had left until after they got the information they were after.

It took them a little while to locate the detective who had arrested Billy Martin. When they did, he wasn't all that anxious to talk to them.

"What's your interest?" Detective William Palmer asked, frowning at Chiun as if he couldn't figure him out.

"We detest child killers," Chiun said.

"Oh, yeah?" Palmer said. "How do you feel about someone who would kill his own parents while they were asleep?"

"Was that proven?" Remo asked.

"If you know anything about this case, you know that it never was, but it would have been if we had been able to get him to court. It's better this way, though."

"Why?" Chiun asked.

"Because somebody saved the city a lot of money by killing the little bastard, and I'm all for that."

Remo stepped in before Chiun could reduce the detective to something less attractive than he already was.

"My friend just doesn't like to see any child killed," he explained.

"Child? Billy Martin wasn't a child," Palmer said, screwing up his already ugly face. It was a mass of bumps and creases that successfully disguised his age, which could have been anywhere between thirty and sixty. "This was a snot-nosed little bastard with absolutely no regard for human life. He got what he deserved.'' He looked directly at Chiun and added, ''You can tell your friend that.''

The detective turned and walked to the rear of the squad room, apparently finished talking with them, but Remo wasn't finished with him.

''Chiun, wait for me here so I'll have a chance to get something useful out of him.''

Chiun snorted and studied the ceiling while Remo headed for the detective's desk.

Palmer was already engrossed in paperwork when Remo approached him, but he looked up when Remo's shadow fell on his desk. ''What's with your Chinese friend?'' he asked. ''Is he some kind of bleeding heart?''

''He's not Chinese, he's Korean.''

Palmer shrugged and said, ''Same thing.''

''Don't let him hear you say that,'' Remo warned. ''He's even more sensitive about that than he is about child killing.''

Palmer looked past Remo at Chiun and said, ''What the hell could he do?''

''Let's not go into that now. I want to talk a little more about the Martin kid.''

Palmer sighed heavily and then said, ''All right. I'll tell you another reason why I'm glad somebody chopped him up into little pieces.''

''Please do.''

''He was gonna get off.''

''You're assuming he was guilty.''

''Hell, man, I know he was guilty. He didn't make any secret of it.''

''He confessed?''

"Not formally, but he didn't do much to deny it, either."

"Then why was he going to get off?"

"He was going to buy his way off by giving some information on something big he said was going down."

"What?"

Palmer shrugged and said, "He never got to it, but he claimed it was really big."

"Any guesses?"

"I don't deal in guesses, mister," the detective said, "I've got too many facts to juggle."

"I guess you do. Can you tell who the lawyer was that bailed him out?"

"What are you, a private dick or something?"

"Something."

"Hell, it's no skin off my nose," Palmer said. "Here." He wrote something on a pad, ripped off the top sheet, and handed it to Remo.

"That's the guy. A loser. I still wonder where he got the money from."

Remo took the slip of paper and said, "If I find out, I'll let you know."

"Yeah, you do that," Palmer said. "You do that."

Chiun was quiet during the ride to the lawyer's office, which made his pupil suspicious. "This is the place," Remo said, pulling up in front of the address Palmer had given him. "Weems. Harvey Weems. Sounds like someone who should be related to old Elmo Wimpler, remember, Chiun?"

Chiun maintained a stony-faced silence, indicating

to Remo that something was definitely going on inside his head.

"Well, let's go and pay him a visit," he said, getting out of the car. Studying the building, he added, "Can't be the world's most successful lawyer, not if he's got his office in this dump."

"You assume," Chiun said, and they'd been all through that before too.

"I'm sorry, Little Father," Remo said. "I should not assume that a pig is a pig simply because it lives in a pigsty."

Chiun declined to comment, which was just fine with Remo. He was hoping they'd find this "child killer" quickly just so Chiun would get off his soapbox.

They went inside the four-story building and learned from the directory that Weems's office was on the fourth floor. In fact, it was the only occupied office on that floor, and one of only four occupied offices in the entire building.

In the absence of an elevator, they began to climb the stairs, which seemed to be more a popular location for excretory functions than anything else. In fact, on the second landing they came across a man who was relieving his bladder in a corner, and Remo asked apprehensively, "You wouldn't be Harvey Weems, the attorney, would you?"

"Shit, no," the man said, shaking off the last few drops and tucking himself away, "I'm Blackie Danelo, the brain surgeon." Giving Remo a disgusted look and Chiun a look of disbelief, the brain surgeon walked past them, descended to the first level, and exited to the street.

Chiun gave Remo a glare that could charbroil a hamburger and preceded him up the remainder of the steps to the fourth level.

"I just asked," Remo said, following.

They scanned the doors on the fourth floor and finally found the one that read HARVEY WEEMS. AT OR EY-AT- AW.

"This is it," Remo said. "At-or-ey at-aw."

When Chiun did not even reply with a glare, Remo knocked on the door. When there was no immediate reply, he knocked a second time.

"Try the doorknob," Chiun suggested as if talking to a child.

"I was about to."

Remo reached for the doorknob and found that it turned freely. He pushed the door open and peered inside the dark office.

"Light," Chiun said.

"Don't you just hate it when someone keeps telling you to do something a split second before you're about to do it anyway?" Remo asked nobody in particular. He flicked on the light and stepped into the room, which turned out to be an outer office with no windows. Across from them was another door, which presumably led to the at-or-ey's office.

"Let's see if he's in there," Remo said.

"Someone is," Chiun said.

"Oh?"

"You do not smell it?"

Remo stopped and sniffed the air, and damned if he didn't smell it. Blood, sharp and acrid, accompanied by the odor of death. Somebody was in there, all right, and whoever it was wasn't about to open the door for them—or anybody.

He walked across the room and opened the door. The room was dimly lit by a shaft of light coming through the lone window. He switched on the light, knowing what he would find.

There was blood everywhere, on the walls, the floor, the desk, the window. The body was not immediately noticeable, which meant it had to be behind the desk.

Three long strides across the room confirmed his guess.

"Whew" he said, "looks like the blade men got here ahead of us."

Chiun came over to examine the body, which had been hacked almost to pieces.

"Weems," he said.

"Maybe," Remo said. "Are you assuming?"

"I do not assume," Chiun said stiffly, "I employ logic. This is Weems's office, Weems's desk—"

"And that makes it Weems? That's logic."

Chiun closed his eyes and continued. "This man has his jacket and shoes off. The jacket is on the back of the desk chair, and the shoes are underneath the desk. Who else would make himself that comfortable?"

Remo shrugged and said, "Maybe you're right."

"Get his wallet."

Remo checked the jacket on the back of the chair, and when that did not yield a wallet, he checked the dead man's pants, coming up with a faded brown leather billfold.

"Driver's license," he said, extracting same from the wallet. Reading the name on the license aloud, he said, "Harvey Weems." He put the license away, replaced the wallet, and said, "And I'm Dr. Watson."

"This man cannot help us."

"Good observation."

"We must, however, determine why he was killed."

"I'll bite. Why was he killed?"

"He knew something."

"Ah."

Chiun looked at the top of the desk and noticed a pad with some writing on it. A large dollar figure inside a heart, and a smaller figure next to it. Also the words "phone" and "man's voice" scribbled on the pad.

"There," Chiun said, pointing.

Remo looked at the pad and said, "The larger figure is the amount of the bail."

"And the smaller?"

"Ten percent," Remo said. "Probably his fee for posting the bail."

"And the words?"

Remo read them, then said, "He got his instructions from a man's voice over the phone. This guy didn't know who went for the bail."

"Perhaps he did," Chiun said, "and he was not supposed to."

"And that's why he was killed?"

"A possibility."

"A good one," Remo admitted grudgingly. "You may out-Holmes Holmes yet, Chiun."

"I do not know this Holmes you refer to, but that

is no matter. It is a reasonable assumption that this man discovered who had supplied the bail, and either that information or what he tried to do with it got him killed.''

"Blackmail?"

"A possibility."

"Then whoever killed the kid killed him as well," Remo said, quickly adding, "I'm not assuming, mind you."

"No, simply stating another possibility," Chiun said.

"Right," Remo said. "I guess we might as well take a look around . . . see if we can find anything helpful."

Remo started going through the dead man's desk while Chiun simply strolled about the room, looking at nothing but seeing everything.

Remo finally found something useful in the top drawer of a file cabinet, the only drawer that wasn't empty.

"This guy wasn't exactly overburdened with cases," he said, pulling out the case files. Sifting through them, he came up with one on Billy Martin.

"A file," he said.

"Containing what?"

He opened it and found some newspaper clippings and one sheet of paper. On the paper was what appeared to be the kid's home address.

"This must be the scene of the crime," Remo said, holding the paper up.

"The child's address," Chiun said. Every time he called the Martin kid a "child," Remo actually winced.

"Yeah, the kid's address," he said, dropping the folder on the desk. "I guess we'd better try there next."

He closed the folder and then replaced it in the drawer.

"After we leave, I'll find a pay phone. . . ." Remo started to say, but then he had second thoughts.

"Yes?" Chiun asked, giving him an arched eyebrow.

"If we call the cops, they'll be looking for us because Palmer knows we came here. We'll have to avoid that as long as possible."

"We will go directly to the child's house," Chiun said. "Perhaps there we can find something that will help me avenge his untimely death and prevent the deaths of other children."

Remo didn't quite agree with Chiun's reasoning, but at least they agreed on what their next move should be.

CHAPTER FOUR

Using a map supplied by the rental agency, Remo finally located the neighborhood where the kid's house was. Remo was surprised because he was expecting a slum. What he found was a better-than-middle-class section of town and a nice, neat, expensive house with an equally expensive car in the driveway.

"Not what I expected," he said, stopping the car behind the expensive model.

"Do not expect anything, and you will never be disappointed," Chiun said.

"Right," Remo said. "Let's take a look."

As they started up the walk of the house, a neighbor came out of the house next door and stared at them. The neighbor was a small man with a hangdog look on his face, who looked to be in his mid-fifties. Remo just knew that there was an overbearing, money-grubbing wife in the house somewhere.

"Hello," Remo said.

"Hello. If you're looking for the people who live in that house, you're not going to find them."

At least we don't have to try and get him to talk, Remo thought.

"Oh? Why is that?"

"They're dead."

"Dead? How did that happen?"

"Don't you read the papers?"

"We're from out of town," Remo said.

The man looked past Remo at Chiun and then confided, "I would have guessed that about him."

"You're very observant."

"That's what everyone tells me."

"You probably know more about what happened here than I could have found out by reading the papers anyway."

"You're right."

"So what happened?"

"The kid, Billy, he went crazy and killed them."

"Who?"

"His parents. He beat them to death with a tire iron while they were asleep."

"That's awful."

"It sure is, but nobody around here was really surprised about it."

"Why not?"

The man shrugged and said, "He was just that kind of kid, you know? See that car in the driveway?"

"Expensive machine," Remo said.

"That was the kid's. He drove it all the time, and he wasn't even old enough to drive."

"Is that right?"

"On top of it all, he had friends who did the same thing, you know. Drove expensive cars even though they weren't old enough to have licenses. And they were over all the time."

"I see. How long did the Martins live here?"

"Actually, they only moved in a couple of months ago. I think the father—Allan, his name was—got a raise or something from the company he worked for."

"What company was that?"

"An automobile company, what else? I think it was National Motors. Yeah, that's it."

"He must have gotten a large raise."

The neighbor made a face. "Nah, they were flashing more money than he could have gotten just from a raise."

"You noticed that, did you?"

"How could I help it, what with that car and all? Maybe they came into an inheritance or something."

"I guess that's possible."

"Especially since they paid cash for the house."

"That *is* a lot of money to flash," Remo agreed, wondering if there was anything this man didn't know. Maybe he'd ask him who killed the kid.

"So you don't really know where all the money came from, then?" he asked.

"Hey, I'm not nosy."

"I can see that," Remo said. "Just observant."

"Right, that's what everybody says."

That's because they're too polite to say "nosy," Remo thought.

"So what happened to the son after he murdered his parents?" Remo asked.

"That's the funny part," the neighbor said, and Remo could feel Chiun stiffen behind him.

"Funny?" Remo said.

"Yeah. You see, the police arrested him, and a judge let him out on bail. Less than an hour later, Billy Martin was dead. Somebody killed *him*."

"Really? That must have been a shock."

"Especially to him," the man said, and then laughed at his own joke. Remo just hoped that Chiun would be able to keep himself under control.

"So now they're all dead," Remo said.

"Looks that way."

"Daaa-vid!" a woman's voice called from inside the neighbor's house.

"Oops, there's the Mrs.," David said. "I've got to go in and tighten a faucet or something. Listen, I didn't ask you—why were you looking for the Martins?"

"Oh," Remo said, "I was just going to try and sell them a set of encyclopedias."

"Oh, yeah?"

"I don't suppose you'd want to buy—"

"Oh, I couldn't. My Mrs. would kill me. Well, better luck with someone else."

"Thanks."

When the neighbor went back into his house, Remo could feel Chiun take a deep breath behind him.

"I do not know how I can stand to be among you people," Chiun said. "There is no sensitivity, no warmth, no pity for a child cut down in the prime of life. There is—"

"—Someone in the house," Remo said, cutting Chiun off.

"What?"

Pointing, Remo said, "There's someone in the Martin house, and the house is supposed to be vacant. I'm going to take a look."

"Now we have to break into the home of a dead child," Chiun said despairingly.

"Somebody already beat us to it." Remo said.

"For once, you are right." The old Korean started for the house. Remo hurried after him.

"Let's just hope no one calls the cops," Remo said as they reached the front door. "You want me to break it down?"

Chiun made a rude nosie, reached forward, and effortlessly forced the door open with the touch of one hand. "Only a pale piece of pig's ear would break down the door of a dead child's home," he said in disgust.

"When I said 'break,' I didn't mean '*break*'. . . ." Remo started to explain, but then decided to let it go. "Let's see who's inside."

The front door opened right into the living room, which was empty. There were a couple more rooms on the first level—kitchen, family room or den—and they were empty too.

"Upstairs," Chiun said.

"Good guess."

"I heard—"

"I know, I heard it too," Remo assured his mentor. Someone was walking around on the second floor, walking without stealth, because whoever it was thought the house was empty. The rooms on the first floor were intact, so if the intruder was searching, he was doing a decent job of it.

"Let's go up and see who it is," Remo said, starting for the stairs.

"I will wait here," Chiun said.

Remo started up the steps without arguing. Chiun obviously had something on his mind, and Remo decided to leave him alone with it.

Upstairs, he went through the first bedroom, then found the intruder in the bathroom, gong through the medicine cabinet.

The man was tall, with curly brown hair and very pale skin, as if he had been ill or had never been introduced formally to the sun.

"Do you prefer aspirin or Tylenol?" Remo asked.

The man started violently, knocking a couple of plastic vials into the sink as he turned to look at Remo. His eyes immediately caught Remo's attention. They were dark, deep set, and very intense, with a lot of white showing. There was no way to tell if that was their normal state, or merely a manifestation of the man's surprise.

"Who are you?" the man demanded. His voice was deep and very authoritative, as if he were used to being obeyed without question.

"I was about to ask you the same question," Remo replied.

"You have no right to be here."

"And you do, I suppose."

"I have every right," the man said. He turned, retrieved the vials from the sink, replaced them in the medicine cabinet, and slid the door closed.

"How do you figure that?"

"The people who lived here were members of my parish while they were alive."

"Your parish?"

"Yes. My name is Lorenzo Moorcock. I am the minister of the Church of Modern-day Beliefs."

"And what are you doing here if you know that the people who lived here are dead?"

"I came to cleanse the house."

"Are things so bad that you've got to take in house cleaning on the side?"

"Levity is for fools."

"And jail is for burglars, bozo," Remo said, grabbing Moorcock by the collar. "So 'fess up. What are you doing here?"

"In order for the souls of these dear departed members of my parish to find peace, their home must be cleansed of evil spirits," the minister said hurriedly, gasping for air. "Especially considering the way they died."

"So you were cleansing the medicine chest and the toilet?" Remo asked, releasing the man. "Seems to me a can of Ajax would do the job just as well, and you could leave God out of it. I'm sure he has a pretty full schedule . . . but then you'd know more about that than I would."

Moorcock fixed Remo with a piercing stare—his eyes really were like that all the time—and said, "We do not speak of God in my church." He walked past Remo out of the bathroom into the bedroom.

"You don't talk about God?"

"We are too modern for that," the minister said haughtily.

"That's interesting."

"If you are truly interested, you may come to my church and listen to me preach," Moorcock said. "If you merely intend to scoff, you are welcome nonetheless."

"I'll put on my scoffing shoes and take you up on that," Remo said. "I'd like to see a church where they don't talk about God."

Moorcock turned and headed for the stairs.

"If you happen to see a little Oriental gentleman downstairs, tell him that we already spoke, and he won't detain you."

"An Oriental?"

"Yes."

"He is not a heathen, is he?"

"No, he's Korean."

Moorcock frowned at Remo, then turned and went down the steps to the first floor. Remo went back into the bedroom.

He searched the entire second floor and found nothing. He was certain that Reverend or Minister Moorcock had not left with anything substantial, unless there was something in one of the pockets of his worn jeans. Apparently, his congregants not only did not talk about God, but they had some new ideas about how men of the cloth should dress.

Remo went back downstairs to see if Chiun had come up with anything. He found the little Oriental standing virtually as he had left him.

"Did you search?" he asked.

"No."

"You mean I've got to do it myself? Chiun, you better come out of this funk you're in."

"I merely meant . . ."

"Let me look around, and then you can tell me what you've been doing while I've been working."

Chiun opened his mouth to say something but quickly closed it again and watched as Remo searched the rooms on the first floor of the house. Remo came back empty-handed.

"You know," Remo said, "I don't know what we've been looking for, but I haven't come up with anything remotely resembling it."

"Have you finished searching?"

"Yeah, I'm done. Damned if I can find anything that would help."

"You will if you go over to that corner of the living room," Chiun said, pointing with one long, tapered, wrinkled finger.

Remo stared for a moment and then said, "That corner?"

Chiun nodded. "As I might have expected, you passed by the obvious."

Remo walked to the indicated corner. "The obvious, huh?"

"Reach above you."

Remo put his arms up and found that the ceiling was a few inches beyond his fingertips.

"Stand on something," Chiun said wearily.

Remo pulled over a small footstool, stood on it, and said, "Now what?"

"If you'll look above you, you will see that there

are very faint finger marks on the ceiling tile immediately above your head.''

Remo looked up quickly and saw that Chiun was right. There were *very* faint marks resembling fingerprints.

''Match your fingers with those marks and lift the tile, and perhaps we will find something helpful.''

Remo reached up, touched the tile, and lifted it easily. Something fell out and fluttered to the floor.

It was a fifty-dollar bill.

''Isn't that interesting?'' Remo said, looking from the bill to Chiun. The old Oriental jabbed his finger at the ceiling. Remo stuck his hand into the opening and began pulling out banded stacks of bills.

''This is even more interesting,'' he said as each stack thudded to the floor.

When he pulled out the last one, he slipped the tile back into place, got down off the footstool, and began gathering the money up, then piled the bills on a coffee table.

''How much is there?'' Chiun asked, coming over to look.

''A lot,'' Remo said. ''I don't think the exact amount is all that important. I'm just wondering what a man who works on an auto assembly line is doing with an extra fifty, let alone this much of a stash.''

''Put it back,'' Chiun said.

''Back?''

''Do you want to take it with you in your pockets?''

Remo paused, remembering a time when the answer might have been yes. ''No, I guess there's no need to lug it along with us, unless Smitty wants it.''

"It will go to the dead child's family," Chiun said. "Put it back."

"Anything to keep you from starting that child stuff again," Remo said.

He climbed up on the stool, but when Chiun refused to hand him the money, he had to get down, gather up a few stacks, put them back, and then repeat the process until all of the bills were back in the ceiling hideaway.

"Did you meet the minister when he was leaving?" Remo asked.

"We introduced ourselves," Chiun said.

"We're going to have to take a look at his church before this is over."

"Is there something unusual about it?"

"Yeah, they don't talk about God there."

"Most unusual," Chiun said. "What do they talk about?"

"I don't know," Remo said, looking up at the ceiling tile.

There was little more they could learn from the house, and the approaching darkness hinted that it was time to leave. Outside, they found a group of kids—fifteen- and sixteen-year-old boys, actually—congregated around their car.

"They either want to mug us or tell us who killed Billy Martin," Remo said to Chiun.

"They are children," Chiun reminded his student. "They must not be harmed."

"I'll try and remember that."

As they approached the group, Remo wondered if these were the friends that the neighbor had told them about, the ones the Martin kid had hanging around all the time.

"Hey, who's your friend, man?" one of the boys asked.

"He is my pupil," Chiun said.

"Naw, I wasn't talking to you, old man," the youth said. "I was talking to *you*." He pointed to Remo.

"Too bad I wasn't listening," Remo said. "How about moving away from the car?"

"Oh, is this your car?" the same youth asked. He seemed to be the spokesman of the group.

"It belongs to a rental agency, but they don't like nose prints on the window either."

The kid sidestepped to cut Remo off as he approached. He was as tall as Remo, but thinner and lighter. "You're a funny man, ain't you?"

"I'm a patient man," Remo said, "but it's not going to last forever, so don't push your luck."

The boy looked Remo over and wasn't impressed. The man facing him was dark-haired, not overly tall or muscular, and didn't seem to pose an immediate threat. The only unusual things about him were his wrists, which were about as thick as tomato cans, and his choice of friends.

"Is this your father?" the boy asked, grinning.

Remo looked at Chiun, who gave him a warning look back. Remo took a deep breath and turned his attention back to the young man.

"Look, son, if you've got something particular on your mind, I wish you'd get to it. Otherwise, you can just get out of our way."

"Oooh," the kid said, widening his eyes and backing up a step. "Tough talk when all you've got to back you up is one old chink."

Remo looked at Chiun to see what effect this remark had had. Maybe it would make him forget that these were just "children." Chiun's face was as impassive as ever, though, so he wasn't going to get any help there.

"What's on your mind?"

"We was just wondering what you were doing in that house, is all. See, our friend used to live there."

"Is that a fact? What if I told you it was none of your business?"

"Well then," the boy said, looking at his friends for support, "I guess we'd just have to make it our business, wouldn't we?"

"Look, I'd appreciate it if you wouldn't get my friend here angry," Remo said, indicating Chiun. "I can't be responsible for his actions if you get him angry."

"Him?" the boy asked, laughing. He looked at his friends, who also laughed on cue. "What could he do?"

"Oh," Remo said, as if he was in pain, "I've seen him do some nasty things to men twice your size. Sometimes he doesn't know his own strength."

"Oh, yeah?" The kid looked at Chiun with keen interest. "What is he, some kind of black belt or something?"

"Black belts cross the street to avoid passing him," Reno said quietly.

The entire group studied Chiun now, and then the

leader said, "Well, what about you? You a black belt? Or maybe just yellow." The others laughed at the leader's joke.

"Clever," Remo said. "Maybe when you grow up, you can be a comedian in the state pen."

The kid stepped forward, blocking the car door with his body. "You ain't getting in this car, man."

"Oh, no?" Remo snatched the car's hood ornament and pulled it free of its mooring. Without taking his eyes off the boy, he squeezed the ornament until the metal began to bend in his hand.

When it had folded in half, he buried it in his palm and closed his hand again. Then, applying constant pressure, the way Chiun had taught him, he managed to grind the metal into a powder resembling salt crystals.

He walked up to the leader of the group and poured the powder over the kid's head. "Time to go, Chiun," he said.

The group fanned out and away from the car, congregating around their leader, who glinted in the sunlight like a statue made of glitter.

"Happy I didn't hurt anybody?" Remo asked, starting the car and pulling away.

"A barely satisfactory performance," Chiun said.

"Oh? I thought I was pretty good."

"There was no need to intimate that I am the possessor of an unmanageable temper."

"Intimate? I didn't intimate. I flat-out lied—"

"Oh, 'how sharper than a serpent's tooth . . .' " Chiun began, permitting a pained look to cross his face.

"Okay, I apologize. Anyway, I'm interested in Moorcock. He was obviously looking for something in the house. What was it?"

"What were we looking for?" Chiun asked.

"I don't know."

"Why could he not have been looking for the same thing?"

"He might have been," Remo said, but he couldn't help but wonder if the good minister hadn't been looking for that money. And where had Billy Martin's father gotten such a windfall?

A man entered the office of a car rental agency and began to tell the clerk behind the desk a story about a terrible driver.

"We very nearly had an accident, and I'd really like to give him a piece of my mind," the man told the clerk.

"I'm terribly sorry, sir. But are you sure he was driving one of our cars?" the clerk asked.

"Positive. The car had one of your stickers in the windshield," the man replied. "I'd like to find out who the guy is and where I can find him."

"Well, it would be highly irregular for me to give out that information, you understand," the clerk said. "And we may not even have a local address for him."

"I understand," the man assured him, surreptitiously pressing a crisp twenty-dollar bill into the clerk's hand.

"What was the license number?"

The man recited the license number of the car. The

clerk looked it up and gave him the man's name—
Remo Randisi—plus the name of the hotel where he
was supposed to be staying.

"Thank you very much. I appreciate this . . .
more than you know."

The man left the rental agency and crossed the
street to a large black car. He got into the back,
where another man was waiting for him, and repeated the information he'd gotten from the clerk.

"Very good," the other man said. "Now we'll
handle this Remo, whoever he is."

"Do you think he's a cop?" the first man asked.

"If he is," the second man said, "he's a dead
one."

CHAPTER FIVE

In the morning, Remo's car exploded.

He wasn't in it. No one was, and he didn't find out about it until he came down to the hotel parking lot. Chiun was up in their room composing that same damned Ung poem, and he'd decided to leave him to his artistic expression while he checked out some leads. He was in no mood to listen to Chiun harp about "children" again.

There was a fire truck outside the hotel, and a hose had been run into the parking area beneath the building. Whem Remo got off the elevator at the parking lot level, he saw all the commotion and collared a hotel employee to ask what had happened.

"Some car just exploded, Mac," the guy said. He was one of the parking valets and had in fact parked Remo's car for him the night before.

"Which car?" Remo asked.

The man took a second look at Remo and then said, "Well, I'll be damned if it wasn't yours."

"Mine, huh?" Remo said. "Do they know how it happened?"

"I don't think so. I ain't heard nothing yet."

"But you will, won't you?" Remo asked, slipping the guy a five spot. "Eventually you'll hear all about it?"

"I sure will, mister."

"Well, there's ten more in it for you if I hear about it right after you do."

"You got it."

"Good. Do you think you could go out front and have a cab meet me there? I forgot something upstairs."

"Sure, my pleasure."

Remo took the elevator up one flight and got off at the lobby. He didn't want to be seen walking through the garage with all the ruckus that was going on, and he didn't want to have to take the time to answer questions. As it was, the police were bound to find out that the car had been rented by him, and he'd be answering their questions soon enough. Right now, however, he had a few of his own to get answered.

The cab was waiting out front. He got in and told the driver to take him to the National Motors plant. He was going there to talk to some of the people who worked with Allan Martin, Billy's father.

During the ride, he contemplated the possibility that his rented car had blown up for some reason other than that somebody wanted it to—preferably with him in it. After all, if someone had indeed planted a bomb, they'd done a rotten job because the thing had gone off prematurely . . . luckily for him. Still, that was the likeliest explanation. At least whoever had done it had saved him the trouble of trying to explain to the rental agency what had happened to the hood ornament.

At the plant Remo presented himself to the girl at the reception area, who was in charge of dispensing security clearance badges to visitors. The girl was young and very pretty, with long blond hair and green eyes. And she was obviously interested in Remo. It took little more than flattery and a few gentle touches, strategically placed where Sinanju had taught him women were vulnerable—for him to appropriate a pass that gave him the right to go anywhere in the plant. He also managed to squeeze out of her the name of Allan Martin's immediate superior. It was Jack Boffa, the assembly line foreman.

"You make sure you stop back this way before you leave," she said hopefully when he was through with her.

"Of course," he said in his most charming manner. "I'll have to return the badge, won't I?"

He wandered through the plant until he was finally able to locate the assembly line, taking the time to observe how the thing was run.

From what he could see, more than a few of the men working the line were pretty drunk, and the ones who weren't drunk were pretty damned sloppy. Unlike Japan, where auto workers took great pride in their work and everyone on the assembly lines sang the company song and committed *seppuku* if one car was defective—or so he had heard—this looked like the kind of outfit where they called it a good day's work if no more than half of the cars manufactured were recalled for potentially fatal defects.

It was enough to make one seriously consider taking up bicycle riding.

Off to one side he spotted a man who had to be Jack Boffa. He was a tall, solidly built man standing with his arms folded across his chest and a clipboard dangling from one hand. Remo knew that a clipboard always signified authority.

"Excuse me," he said, approaching the foreman.

The man looked at Remo, frowned when he didn't recognize him, and asked, "How did you get in here?"

"I'm authorized," Remo said, touching his badge.

"I guess you are," the man replied, studying the plastic square on Remo's jacket. "What can I do for you?"

"Are you Jack Boffa?"

"That's me."

"Things are run a little loose around here, aren't they?"

Boffa's head swiveled, and he looked hard at Remo. "What are you, an inspector or something? We usually get some kind of warning. We pay enough—"

"Hold it. I'm not an inspector."

The tension eased from the man's face, and he said, "Well, then, who are you?"

"Somebody interested in what happened to Allan Martin and his family."

"Jesus, that's no secret. Him and his old lady were killed by their own son, and then the boy got himself killed."

"I'm interested in why the boy killed his parents, and who killed the boy afterward."

"I can't help you with that, mister. I ain't no cop."—

Remo caught the look Boffa was giving him then and said, "I'm not a cop either, but I'd still like to ask you a few questions."

"What are you, private heat?"

"Something like that."

"I don't know much," the foreman said with a shrug.

"You knew Martin, didn't you?"

"Yeah, like I know my other workers. There was something, though."

"Like what?"

"Well, the last few months, Al Martin seemed a little jumpy, you know? Like something was really bothering him."

"Did you ask him about it?"

"Once, yeah. I'm interested in anything that keeps my men from working at peak efficiency, you know?"

Remo cast a dubious glance at the men on the assembly line and said, "That's obvious. What did Martin say it was?"

"Nothing. He said nothing was wrong at all."

"You didn't press him?"

"He did his work. If he wanted me to mind my own business, that was okay with me."

"Did he get a big raise anytime during the past few months?"

"A raise? You kiddin'? If he had gotten a raise, do you think he would have been so jumpy? Naw, ain't nobody around here gotten a raise in months, and nobody has gotten a big raise in years. That just ain't company policy."

Remo was about to cut off the conversation when he thought of something else.

"These cars you're working on now—where are they being shipped when they're done?"

"This lot?" the man asked. He consulted his clipboard and said, "They're earmarked for New York, New Orleans, and Los Angeles."

Remo nodded and said, "You mind if I talk to some of your men?"

"As long as you don't keep them from their work."

"I'll try not to," Remo said wryly.

"As a matter of fact, if you try that section there," the foreman said, pointing, "they're just about ready to go on a break."

"Thanks for your help."

"Sure."

Remo walked over to the section the foreman had indicated and saw that three or four men were pulling off their gloves. He decided to follow them into the lounge.

He loitered outside the door, waiting for the men to get settled, and then entered the lounge. The four men had paired off at two different tables, which was all right with him. He didn't want anyone's uncooperative attitude rubbing off on anyone else.

"Excuse me," he said, approaching two of the men, who were holding Styrofoam cups of coffee. The two at the other table were passing a flask back and forth.

"What can we do for ya?" one of the men asked.

"I'm looking into the death of Al Martin and his family, and I was wondering if I could ask you a couple of questions."

"What's to ask?" the other man asked. He was the bigger of the two, with a scar that bisected his shaggy right eyebrow. The other man was smaller and rail thin. "Al and his wife was killed by their kid, and nobody knows—or cares—who killed him."

"I care," Remo said. "I'd like to know why Billy Martin killed his parents."

"We can't help you," the man with the scar said, looking down into his coffee.

"Can't or won't?"

"Take your pick, mister," the thin man said. He looked at Remo for a moment, then nervously averted his eyes. Remo was sure that it wasn't he who was making the man nervous, but his questions.

He decided to try the other two men before forcing someone to talk to him. "Thanks," he said to the men, who merely grunted in return.

Remo left them to their coffee and walked to the table where the two men were sharing a flask. Both of these men were much like the man with the scar, large and not very bright looking. He didn't expect to have better luck with them, but he was willing to give it a try.

"Excuse me," he said. When the two men looked

at him quizzically, he tried the same opening gambit on them.

"Can't help ya," one of the men said, and the other man nodded his agreement.

"Aren't you interested in why Martin was killed?"

"He was killed by that crazy kid of his," the man said, while his buddy continued to nod. "Now, look, get out of my face. I'm trying to talk with my friend here."

He reached out to accept the flask from his friend, but Remo got to it first.

"How do you think an inspector would like to find out that you men are drinking on the job?"

"You're looking for trouble, mister," the man said, standing up, "and I'm just the guy that can give it to you."

The man was much larger and heavier than Remo and obviously felt that this gave him a distinct advantage.

"Is this your flask?" Remo asked.

The man seemed surprised at the question. "Yeah, it's mine."

"Nice one," Remo said. "Sturdy, isn't it?" As he said it, Remo poked a hole in the metal container with his little finger, and the whiskey started to run out onto the floor.

"Oh, I'm sorry," he said. "I guess it wasn't as sturdy as I thought."

"What the hell . . ." the man said, taking the flask back and studying the hole. "How'd you do that?"

"I've got sharp nails," Remo said.

"You ruined my flask!" the man said aloud, and the other two men in the room looked up.

"You need help, Lou?" the man with the scar called.

"This guy's a wise guy," Lou answered. "He's asking a lot of questions, and he ruined my flask."

Remo heard two chairs scrape back behind him but kept his eyes on the man named Lou. "Look, fellas, all I need is a few simple answers to a few simple questions. I don't want any trouble."

"Mister, that's just what you bought," Lou said, prodding Remo's chest with his forefinger. His friend stood up and nodded his agreement.

"That's not a nice thing to do," Remo said, looking down at the man's finger, briefly considering breaking it. "How would you like it if I did that to you?" he asked.

To demonstrate, he showed the man his forefinger and then poked him in the chest with it. The man shot back across the room as if yanked from behind by a rope and crashed into the coffee machine. He fell to the floor in front of it, and the machine dumped a cup with heavy cream and sugar on his head in alternate streams of black and white.

"Hey," Lou's friend said, speaking for the first time. The two men behind Remo each grabbed an arm, and the third man pushed the table out of the way so he could front Remo.

The rail-thin man had taken hold of Remo's left arm, so Remo lifted his arm and hit the man in front of him with the thin man as if he were a club.

"Jesus," the man with the scar said. Remo looked

at him, and the man released his right arm in a hurry.

Remo's right hand shot out and grabbed the man by the throat, lifting him off the ground. "Now let me ask my questions again, and we'll see if I can't get a couple of answers. Okay?"

The man tried to nod, but that only tightened the grip Remo had on his throat.

"Do you know anything about Al Martin coming into a lot of money over the past few months?"

"I can't tell you nothing, mister," the man rasped.

"Can't or won't?" Remo asked.

"I can't! I don't know nothing, I swear!"

"He doesn't know anything," the man named Lou said, using the coffee machine to help himself to his feet. "Neither do they."

"Oh, really?" Remo said. He opened his hand and allowed the man with the scar to fall to the floor. "What about you? What do you know?"

The man averted his eyes and said hastily, "Me—I don't know nothing either. Uh, none of us does. If Al Martin was flashing a lot of money, we don't know nothing about it."

"And nobody else came into a lot of money?"

"I guess not."

"Why was Martin nervous the past few months?"

Lou shrugged and said, "Maybe he was worried about that crazy kid of his. Maybe he knew the kid was planning to murder him. Who knows?"

"Yeah," Remo said, "Who knows?"

Remo looked around the lounge, where three men

were still on the floor and Lou was leaning on the coffee machine.

"You guys better clean up," he said. "Your break must be just about over."

On the way out he had to pass Lou and the coffee machine, so he asked one more question. "Where do you think Al Martin could have gotten a lot of money?"

"Jesus, mister," the guy said, "maybe he made some overtime, or maybe the company gave him some extra pay because nobody died in one of the cars he worked on. You know, incentive pay?"

"Incentive pay," Remo said. "Maybe you can get the company to give you some incentive pay, Lou. You know, to buy a new flask with."

He turned to the other men in the room, said, "Gee, thanks for all your help, guys," and left.

CHAPTER SIX

Remo left the National Motors plant, touching the pretty receptionist in a way she wouldn't soon forget as he returned his badge. Then he grabbed a cab and instructed the driver to keep his meter running and wait for orders.

"Jessir," the Puerto Rican cabbie said, happily switching the meter on.

It wasn't long until the end of the shift. Remo kept his eye out for his old friend Lou. Pretty soon he saw Lou behind the wheel of an expensive-looking sports car, and knew that he'd made the right decision.

"Follow that car," he told the cabbie.

"The jazzy red one?"

"That's the one."

"Jou got eet," the cabbie said, and roared away from the curb.

"Don't lose him, but don't let him know we're here, either," Remo said.

"Don' jou worry."

In about twenty minutes Remo found himself in a neighborhood reminiscent of the one the Martin family had lived in. He watched as Lou pulled his car into the driveway of a neat little house, and then told the cabbie to pull over and wait.

"Jou not gonna keel him, are jou?" he asked Remo.

"No, I'm not going to kill him. Why?"

"If you keel him, it's double the meter."

A law-abiding citizen, Remo thought, "I won't be long," he said.

"Take your time."

Remo approached the house that Lou had gone into and walked to the side, searching for a window to look through. He found himself on a huge patio that had obviously cost a small fortune to build, and peered into the house through a large picture window.

He watched as Lou kissed his wife hello and asked her what was for dinner, and then he saw a kid about fifteen years old come into the room and immediately get into an argument with his old man. You didn't have to be a genius to figure out that Lou was in exactly the same situation that Allan Martin had been in, and he wondered if good old Lou was afraid of ending up the same way.

Making his way back to the cab, Remo knew that his logical next move was to find out where Lou had been getting his money, but he had to do it without arousing any more suspicion about himself.

That meant Smitty.

Remembering a pay phone on the corner next to a

small deli, Remo waved the cabbie to keep waiting and walked down the block to the phone. From there he could still see the house while he talked to Smith.

Remo dialed the digits for Folcroft Sanitarium in Rye, New York, and then waited to be put through to Smith.

"It's Remo," he said when Smith came on the line.

"I hope you haven't run into a problem," the lemony voice answered.

"You know us, Smitty," Remo said. "Problems we handle by ourselves. I called to ask you a favor."

"What is it?"

"I need somebody checked out. You'll have to get his name from his license plate number."

"What do you want to know?"

"I want to know where he's getting his money." Briefly, he told Smith what they had found inside the Martin house, then said that he felt that the man named Lou was in the same situation.

"He's showing more money than he should, and I want to know where it's coming from. Feed it into those computers of yours and see what they come up with."

"I'll take care of it."

"Good. I'll get back to you for the answer. There's another thing."

"What?"

Remo told Smith about the cars that were being shipped to New York, New Orleans, and Los Angeles by National Motors.

"Those towns ring a bell with you?"

"They certainly do. I'll run the information through the computers and see what they come up with."

"Yeah, thanks. Stay tuned for further details."

Before Smith could answer, Remo hung up.

Lou's kid was leaving the house.

Harold W. Smith addressed himself to the Folcroft computers, feeding in the cities of New York, New Orleans, and Los Angeles and the information Remo had given him. He programmed the machine to report on any common bond that existed between the three major cities. It took only a few moments for the mechanical marvels to come up with an answer, and the response puzzled him.

Why should drug arrests and drug activities be down in all three cities? He double-checked the information he had fed into the machines but the computers still came back with the same answer. Drug arrests in all three cities were down, and down dramatically over recent years.

Smith took off his jacket, seated himself in front of the terminal, and set about trying to learn the connection.

When Remo reached his cab, he woke the driver and said, "Follow that car."

"The red one again?"

"Wait."

They watched as the kid got into the car and pulled out of the driveway.

"That's the one," Remo said. "Hit it."

They followed the kid for about fifteen minutes before the cabbie said, "Uh-oh."

"What's the matter?"

"I don't like where this *cabrone* is heading," the cabbie said. "Bad news, bro."

"Where's he heading?"

"I think he's heading for the ghetto. No fun there, boss."

"Just keep following, buddy. You're getting rich off me; that ought to be worth a risk or two."

"Triple the meter," the cabbie said, stepping on the gas.

After ten more minutes, Remo didn't need the cabbie to tell him where they were. White faces were at a premium on the streets they were now driving through, and the cabbie was becoming increasingly nervous.

Abruptly, the kid pulled his car over to the curb and stopped.

"This guy is *loco en la cabeza* if he leaves that car there, boss."

"Just pull over, friend."

The cabbie pulled over to the curb a few car lengths behind the kid, who was getting out of his car.

"I don't think I'll be needing you anymore," Remo said, sliding over to the curbside. He gave the cabbie a hundred-dollar bill. "Keep the change," he said.

"Jou *loco* too, boss, if jou gonna walk around here."

"I'll take my chances. *Adios.*"

"*Vaya con dios,*" the driver said, and peeled out.

Remo started trailing the kid through the streets, while the denizens of that area gave them both hard looks. The boy didn't seem to notice at all, and Remo just ignored them..

When the boy finally turned down an alley, Remo figured that the kid had reached his destination. Now maybe he'd turn up something he and Chiun could go on.

But when Remo turned to enter the alley, he stopped short because the kid he was following was standing very close to another kid, this one black. They were obviously transacting some business, so he pressed back against the wall and watched.

The conversation got hot and heavy for a few moments, and then an exchange was made. The kid Remo was following handed over an envelope, and the black kid handed over money. It looked like just one thing: a drug deal.

Good old Lou's kid was selling drugs. So that was the connection, Remo thought. Could that have been where Lou was getting his extra money? Had Billy Martin also been dealing in drugs? And was it just the kids, or were the parents involved as well?

As he watched, both kids continued down the alley and then disappeared around a corner. Remo was surprised because the alley appeared to be a dead end. He sprinted after them, and when he reached the corner, he saw that there was a wooden fence with some of the slats missing. The two kids had obviously beat it through there.

Squeezing through the narrow opening, he found himself on a side street. There was no sign of either of the two kids. Cursing, he looked across the street at the buildings, wondering if one or both of the boys could have gone into any one of them. A sign above one of the doorways suddenly caught his eye, and he stared at it in surprise.

It said: THE CHURCH OF MODERN-DAY BELIEFS.

CHAPTER SEVEN

Lorenzo Moorcock was on the podium, delivering an energetic sermon to a somewhat less than energetic-looking flock. Some of them, looking as if they had only come inside to keep warm, were huddled in the rear pews. The more interested flock members were in the front three rows, listening in rapt attention. Remo stood in the back, next to the door, and scanned the pews for any sign of either kid. When he came up empty, he started to listen.

". . . must always remember, dear brothers and sisters, that the old ways are dead. The Father, the Son, the Holy Ghost, the Bible—they are all things of the past and should stay in the past."

Remo wondered why he bothered calling this place a church. Wasn't that an "old" word?

"In the future, we will not even call our meeting place a church," Moorcock said, as if he'd read Remo's mind. "This will simply be the place of meeting."

Catchy, Remo thought.

He went on to talk about something he kept calling "The Satan." In order to modernize their beliefs, he said, they would believe in everything "The Satan" did not believe in. They would advocate free love, abortion, collectivism, and communism. They would look upon the Ayatollah Khomeini as a great man, a great humanitarian, a true leader of the world.

It didn't take Remo very long to figure out that "The Satan" was the United States. It was a term that Khomeini himself was fond of when referring to the United States, and Moorcock was obviously a big Ayatollah booster.

". . . I know I have given you all much food for thought this evening, so I ask you now to go to your homes and contemplate everything I've said. I must also ask you all to stop at the collection plates in the center aisle on your way out and give from your heart. A minimum donation of five dollars is suggested, but feel free to give more."

Remo looked at the collection "plates" on either side of the center aisle and saw two collection "barrels" that looked as large as the ones the forty thieves had hidden in.

He watched as the people left, and damned if everyone who had been sitting in the first three rows didn't drop five bucks or more into the jugs.

Moorcock walked with some people to the rear of the "place of meeting," obviously trying to coax more money out of them. When he saw Remo, he wished his flock members a good evening and approached him.

"You came," he said.

"Apparently."

"To scoff?"

"I came to ask questions."

"Ah, you seek wisdom."

"In a manner of speaking."

"Walk with me," Moorcock said, and started back down the center aisle.

"Aren't you going to take in your collection?"

Moorcock threw a glance at the urns, then said, "No one will steal from me."

"That may not be a modern attitude, but it's different."

"What wisdom do you seek?"

"I'm looking for someone."

"Who?"

"A white kid, about ffteen, or a black kid the same age," Remo said.

"You have no particular preference?" Moorcock asked. Remo saw that his eyes were the same as they had been in the Martin house, dark and intense, with a lot of white showing.

"Either or," Remo said. "There were two of them. One or both might have ducked in here."

"You were chasing them?"

"I was watching them, and I lost them. They came this way."

They reached the front of the church and stopped. Moorcock turned to face Remo.

"They did not come in here."

"Would you tell me if they had?"

"Why were you chasing them?"

"They were consummating a drug deal."

"Are you a policeman?"

"No."

"Why do you care, then? If they, or anyone, wishes to indulge in drugs, why should anyone stop them?"

"Is that one of your modern beliefs?"

"A minor one. That our bodies are ours and we may do what we wish with them."

"Oh, that's good. Original."

"You came to scoff."

"I came here looking for two kids," Remo said with exasperation.

"And I told you they are not here."

Remo considered pressing the self-styled minister a little harder, but at that moment he saw something move behind the man.

"Is there a back door to this place?"

"Yes, but . . ." Moorcock started to say, and then glanced quickly toward it.

"Thanks," Remo said, rushing past him.

Whoever had been hiding behind the rear door was gone. It had to have been one of the two kids, but which one?

It didn't really matter, he decided. The black kid was just a junkie, and the white kid—Lou's kid—he could find again whenever he wanted. Just then he had another idea.

He went back to the alley where the drug deal had been made. Starting from that point, he began to walk the ghetto streets, looking for a junkie or a dealer, whichever came first.

He drew a lot of looks and some *sotto voce* remarks,

but there was something about *this* white man that kept anyone from approaching him. The way he walked, he seemed to be just waiting for someone to make a move on him. The eyes riveted on Remo seemed to say that this was one crazy white dude, and nobody wanted a piece of him.

It wasn't long before Remo found a junkie, a wasted-looking man in his twenties with a runny nose, sitting in a doorway.

"Hey, yo, man," the junkie said. He was so dirty, he might have been white or black. "Got any money, man? A dollar? A dime?"

"Neither one will buy you the high you need, friend," Remo said, crouching down to the junkie's level. "I've got a high you can get without a needle. A high you'll never believe."

"Shit," the junkie said, wiping his nose with the back of his hand.

"I'm serious. But it doesn't come free."

"Aw, man. I ain't got no money," the junkie said in obvious despair.

"This high doesn't cost money."

"You ain't shittin' me? What's it gonna cost me?"

"A name."

"What name? Mine?"

"A dealer."

"Aw, man . . . I can't give up my source." His tone of voice had gone from despair to anguish.

"I don't want your source," Remo said. "I want any source, any name you care to give me."

A cunning glint came into the man's previously dull and listless eyes, and he said, "Anyone?"

"As long as he's a dealer," Remo said. "But if you give me a phony name, I'll come back for you, and instead of a high, I'll give you the worst crash of your life."

Remo touched the junkie briefly, and a shadow of pain crossed his face. It was so fleeting, the pain, that the junkie wasn't even sure he'd felt it, but it prompted the truth from him.

"Try Danny the Man."

"Danny the Man. What's his last name?"

"I don't know. All anybody knows is Danny the Man."

"Where do I find him?"

The junkie gave Remo an address and then gave him directions for getting there.

"Just don't tell him I gave you his name."

"I don't even know yours. But I'll find you if this isn't true."

"It's true, man, it's true," the junkie said, grabbing Remo's arms. "Where's my high, man? You promised!"

"So I did," Remo said. He pulled his arms free of the man's frantic grip, reached around behind him, and touched him on the back of the neck. A euphoric look came over the junkie's face, and he leaned back against the door.

"Oh, wow," he breathed.

"Yeah," Remo said. "You don't know it, but you've just taken the cure. After this, you'll never find another high to match it."

"Oh, wow."

"Thanks for the info."

Remo left the junkie flying high in his doorway and started following the man's directions. The junkie had said it was close enough to walk.

When he reached the building he was looking for, he was surprised to find that it was a fairly decent-looking apartment house, located on the fringes of the ghetto. Close enough to his clientele to deal, but far enough away so that he could persuade himself that he didn't live with them, Remo said to himself.

Here I come, Danny the Man.

Danny "the Man" Lincoln had grown up in the ghetto, and somehow living on the edge of it gave him great satisfaction. He was living there because he wanted to, and he could leave anytime he wanted. He had enough money, and that was something his mother and father never had—enough money to get out.

Danny the Man wasn't expecting company. In fact, he already had company, a willowy black beauty who was stretched out on his bed, awaiting his pleasure and eager to fulfill it.

"Come to bed, Danny."

"What's your hurry, baby?" he asked from the doorway of his bedroom. Of course, he knew what her hurry was. The sooner she made him happy, the sooner she got some "candy," to make her happy. The kind of candy that mainlined you straight to heaven.

"I just want to make you happy, Danny," she said, batting her eyes and dropping the sheet so he could see her full, ripe breasts. "You know how I can make you happy."

"Oh, I know, all right," Danny said.

He was taking off his jacket when there was a knock at the door.

"Now who the hell—"

"Don't answer it," the girl on the bed said. If he answered it, she knew she wouldn't get her fix, and she couldn't wait any longer.

"Just be calm, Laura," he said. "I'll be right back."

He shrugged his jacket back on and walked to the door. There was another knock, and then he reached the door and opened it.

The man who opened the door was tall and black, in his late twenties, wearing a red smoking jacket.

"What can I do for you, my man?"

"Are you Danny the Man?" Remo asked.

"That's me."

"Somebody told me you're a pusher."

Danny laughed and said, "What are you , a cop? Is this a new approach? Get lost, man." The black man started to slam the door, but Remo moved his foot and kept it open.

"I'm not a cop," he said, "I just need to talk to a pusher."

"About what? You looking to get into the business? Everybody wants in on the act."

"That's what I want to talk about," Remo said. He pushed past Danny and entered the apartment.

"Hey, man—"

"You better shut the door, Danny boy, so we don't attract any unwanted attention."

"And how we gonna do that, slick?"

"I'm going to ask you some questions, and if I don't get some straight answers, I'm going to bounce you all over these walls."

"Huh," Danny said contemptuously. It was a demonstration of his contempt that he did shut the door and then folded his arms defiantly. "You're a tough dude, huh? Big man?"

Before Remo could answer, the girl came out of the bedroom, naked.

"Danny—"

"Get back inside, bitch!" Danny the Man snapped.

"Danny, I just need—"

"I got somebody here, stupid. What are you coming out here like that for?"

Looking as if she had just been slapped in the face, she said, "Gee, honey, I just wanted—"

"You just wanted your fix, huh, bitch?" He walked up to her and slapped her viciously across the face. "You don't come walking into a room buck naked when I got company, you dumb cow! Go back in the bedroom and get dressed, and then get the hell out. I don't ever want to see you again!"

"But Danny, I need—"

"I know what you need, and you can go get it from somebody else. But you better have plenty of cash because they might not take a mediocre piece for it like I did."

He gave her a push that propelled her all the way into the next room.

"You're a sweetheart, aren't you?" Remo said.

"She's just a dumb junkie bitch," Danny said.

"In an hour she'll be sitting in some alley someplace sniffling and shaking. She'll give some john a good time for five bucks."

He turned on Remo then and said, "We got some business, huh? You wanna ask me some questions and get straight answers?"

"That's right."

"Well, let's get past that part, white boy, because I want to get to the part where you bounce me off the walls." The black pusher smiled and produced a switchblade from his pocket. He flicked out the blade. "That I gotta see."

The girl came out of the bedroom then, half in and half out of her clothes, crying, but somehow exhibiting a defiance of her own.

"Big man, Danny the Man," she said with contempt. "You ain't a man, Danny boy, you ain't even a good—"

Danny took one step and brought his hand up to deliver a smashing backhand blow that would have rattled the girl's teeth and dislodged some of them if it had landed.

It didn't.

Danny felt an iron grip wrap itself around his wrist, and then he couldn't move his arm at all.

"Not this time," Remo said.

"Let go of my hand," Danny said coldly. He looked as cool as could be, but inside he was wondering what the white man's grip was made of. The man was no bigger than he was, but he couldn't move his goddamn arm!

"Back away from the girl," Remo said, "and then we'll continue our conversation."

Danny the Man's eyes bored into Remo's, and then he took a step back. As Remo let go of his wrist, Danny backed up a couple more steps. The girl, who had flinched in anticipation of the blow, looked at Remo.

"Thanks, mister."

"You'd better leave, miss."

"But, I need—"

"You don't need anything that he can give you," Remo said. "Come on, I'll walk you to the door."

He kept an eye on Danny as he walked with her to the door, and without letting the black drug pusher see what he was doing, he touched the girl on her back, by the fifth vertabra. The girl almost staggered from the jolt of pleasure that shot through her, but he steadied her, opened the door, and guided her into the hall. He left her leaning against the wall, still reeling from her new experience, one she'd never be able to match with any drug.

He closed the door and turned to face Danny, who was staring down at his hands. He was wondering why he had totally forgotten the blade in his left hand when the white man grabbed his right wrist.

"Now, about those questions," Remo said.

"You can ask," Danny said, "but that ain't saying that I'll answer."

"Well, we'll try it the easy way first."

Danny studied Remo for a few moments in silence, then folded up his blade and tucked it away.

"You want a drink?"

"No, thanks. Just some answers."

"Well, go ahead and ask."

The black man walked to a small portable bar, and Remo waited until he had a drink in his hand.

"I want to know about the drug business, Danny," he said. "Specifically in this area."

Danny sipped his drink. "Business ain't exactly booming."

"Why not?"

"There's some new action in town, and it's cutting into business. Not just my business. Everybody's."

"Who are they?"

"We've been trying to find out who's behind it, but all we've been able to find is who the street action is being handled by."

"Don't tell me, let me guess," Remo said. "Kids."

"Yeah, kids," Danny said. "If you know all this, why come to me?"

"Up till now I was just guessing."

"Well, whoever's running these kids is really cutting into our action, and we're looking for a way to fix that. If you can help us out, it would be worth a lot of money to you."

"Sorry, but I've got my own business to worry about."

"Which is?"

"Can't go into that right now, Danny."

"Well, if you can see your way clear to nudging some of these kids off the street while you're taking care of your own business, you could still find a nice chunk of change coming your way."

"I'll keep it in mind."

As Remo started for the door, Danny said, "That's it? That's all you wanted?"

"That's it."

"You mean I gave up an incredible piece of ass for this?" he asked, spreading his arms out helplessly.

"Sorry."

"No big deal," the pusher said. "She's gone, but she'll be back. She needs her candy, and I's de candy man, bro." He showed two rows of gleaming white teeth.

"Maybe she's lost her sweet tooth," Remo said.

CHAPTER EIGHT

Remo left Danny the Man's building. There was no sign of the girl. She had probably gone off somewhere to enjoy her new high.

Anxious to find out if Smith had come up with anything, Remo found a pay phone. It was an old-fashioned booth, with a door and a light that didn't work when he closed it behind him. To his surprise, the phone did work.

He dialed the necessary digits and got Smith on the line.

He didn't notice the group of black youths that was following him.

At the same time a similar group of youths—these white—were moving down the hall toward Remo and Chiun's hotel room. White youths were as unnoticeable in the hotel as blacks were in the ghetto.

There were six of them. Many more, their leader

thought, than would be needed to take care of one old chink.

They clustered around the door and, using the mass of their weight, broke it open and burst into the room.

They were not quite prepared for what met them.

"I've got a common denominator, but I'm not sure I understand it yet," Smith told Remo.

"Tell me about it," Remo said. "We'll figure it out together."

"Well, the figures on drug arrests are down in all three cities," Smith said. "For that to be the case in three major cities in the United States—especially those the size of New York and Los Angeles—is quite improbable. But nevertheless true, according to my computations."

"It's true."

"What do you know?" Smith asked. "Specifically."

"Kids, specifically. This whole thing seems to be about kids."

"Well? Who killed Billy Martin?"

"I still don't know that, but I think I know why he was killed."

"All right, that's a start. Tell me why."

"According to the detective who made the arrest, the Martin kid was promising to spill some pretty big beans in exchange for a deal, but he got killed before he could tell them what it was."

"And you know what it was?"

"I think so. I think what he was going to tell them about was a whole new way of dealing drugs."

"Explain."

"They're using kids—minors—and when these kids get arrested, they go up on juvenile charges, which wouldn't show up in the drug statistics."

"And that's why the figures seem to have gone down."

"Right."

"Then the figures really haven't gone down at all. They just seem to have."

"Right again."

"Well, what good does that do?" Smith asked, puzzled.

"Smitty," Remo said, as if he were talking to a child, "it makes it look like the police are doing a fabulous job. The figures look like they've gone down, and you know police work is all stats. If the stats look good, so do the cops."

"Wait, let me confirm this with the computers while I have you on the line."

"Hey, it's your money," Remo said.

While Smitty played with his machines, Remo became aware of movement outside the phone booth. He was annoyed with himself that he hadn't noticed it earlier. On the sly he checked out the situation; anyone looking into the booth would think he was totally involved with his telephone call.

"This confirms it," Smith said, coming back on the line.

"What does?"

"The computer shows that all of the other juveniles who were killed in those three cities had come into a lot of money recently, and they all had police records.''

"Involving drugs?"

"As you said, it wouldn't show up, but the mere presence of the record and the money is enough to indicate that your supposition is correct.''

"Pretty smart for an assassin, huh?"

"I beg your pardon?" Smith asked.

Remo sighed. Smitty had the sense of humor of a bowling ball. "Forget it. I'm going to break this thing, if only to get Chiun off his somebody-is-killing-the-children-of-the-world kick.''

"He takes that very seriously."

"Chiun takes everything very seriously. Have you got anything yet on that guy I asked you to check out?"

"Not yet."

"Well, I've got something else you can put your machines to work on.''

"What?"

"I want you to run a background check on a minister who calls himself Lorenzo Moorcock. He runs something calld the Church of Modern-day Beliefs, based here in Detroit.''

"What's he got to do with this?"

"I'm not sure. He's flitting around the edge of the whole thing, and I'd like to know more about him.''

"I'll take care of it."

"Good. I'll get back to you."

Remo hung up and knew that the phone booth was

surrounded by a half-dozen surly-looking kids with blades. But what really bothered him was that he knew he was going to have to go through them without killing one, because he'd never hear the end of it from Chiun.

CHAPTER NINE

When Remo got back to his hotel room, the door was open and the place was virtually littered with broken and battered bodies. Chiun was seated peacefully in the midst of the carnage.

"Are they all dead?" Remo demanded accusingly, slamming the door shut behind him.

"Of course. Some of us do not have faulty technique."

"Oh, great," Remo said. He walked around the room checking bodies, hoping to find at least one live one they could question. While doing so, he noticed something that surprised him.

"Chiun, these are all kids," he said. "They're all young, and you killed them."

Chiun made a sound of disgust and said, "You look, but you do not see."

Remo checked the faces again and saw what Chiun meant. Although all of the dead men were young, there wasn't one of them who wasn't of legal age. As far as Chiun was concerned, they were no longer children.

"I guess that's what happens to the kids when they get too old to be pushers," Remo said. "The organization makes them into killers."

"Trash."

"Maybe, but if we'd gotten even one of them alive, we might have found out something."

"Pah," Chiun said. "You left me alone here all day so that my serenity was shattered by these amateurish oafs, and now you bother me with trivialities. You know nothing about suffering."

"I do too. As a matter of fact, I ran into a gang of goons myself."

"You were attacked?"

"Sort of," Remo said, feeling that he had put his foot in his mouth.

"And you questioned them?"

"Well, um, no."

"Yet you didn't kill them?"

"They kind of got away from me." Chiun made a face. "Well, what could I do?" Remo went on. "They were kids, *real* kids. And I knew I'd never hear the end of it from you if I killed even one."

"So what did you do?"

"I scared them away."

"Oh? That's interesting. How?"

"Let's just say we owe the city of Detroit one phone booth."

When the phone rang, Remo raced for it, just to terminate Chiun's questioning.

"Excuse me, Mr. Randisi," the desk clerk said, using the name Remo had registered under.

"Mr. who? Oh, yeah. What is it?"

"There's a policeman here to see you."

"Now?" Remo looked around the corpse-strewn room. "Tell him we're not in."

"I'm afraid he's already on his way up, sir."

"Terrific." Remo sighed. "That's just peachy. His name's Palmer, I suppose."

"Why, yes, sir. He said—"

Remo hung up and ran immediately to the bodies lying sprawled around the room, propping them up on chairs and daubing at the crusted blood on their faces with wet tissues.

"Come on, Chiun. You've got to help make these guys look like they're alive."

"The Master of Sinanju does not perform laborers' tasks," Chiun said.

"But geez, it's the cops," Remo said, dashing frantically to stop one of the bodies as it fell forward off a chair. "They'll pull us in for murder, for Pete's sake. Smitty'll have a hemorrhage."

"I am an assassin," Chiun said loftily. "I do not bring the dead back to life. That is the work of a magician. If Emperor Smith wished evil persons to remain alive, he would not have hired—"

"Grab him, will you?" Remo pointed to the body, which was slowly lolling forward. Chiun flung out his left arm. There was the crunch of neckbones as the body jolted back into an upright position.

Detective Palmer pounded on the door.

"Hold it a second," Remo yelled irritably while

pressing together the skin on another dead man's forehead to cover a hole made by Chiun's index finger.

Softly Chiun spoke. "You had better answer the door."

"I will, already."

"You had better answer it now." Chiun was staring at the door, Remo followed the old man's gaze. The door was falling forward.

"The hinges came off during my altercation with these persons," the old Oriental said. "For aesthetic purposes, I reattached them to the wall."

Indeed, the hinges were embedded beautifully in the plaster. The only trouble was that they weren't attached to anything.

Remo rushed for the door, stopped it before it slammed to the floor, and righted it. Then, using a lot of muscle, he creaked it open a hair as if he were opening it normally.

"Nice," Palmer said.

Remo shook his head. "I've been calling the hotel maintenance department for hours."

Palmer tried to peek through the narrow opening. "Mind if I come in?"

"Yes," Remo said emphatically. "That is, we were asleep. We're not dressed for entertaining."

"I just counted six guys in there."

"Well . . ." Remo thought for a moment. "They're asleep too."

The detective gave Remo a disgusted look. "Oh, I get it. A pajama party."

"Ummm . . ."

Chiun's wrinkled face peered out beneath Remo's elbow. "Silence, please," he hissed. "I am conducting a séance. My associates are in deep trance." The face ducked and vanished.

Palmer folded his arms over his chest. "Okay," he said. "What the hell's going on here?"

"Shhh," Remo whispered. "You heard him. The trancees can't be disturbed."

Palmer tried again to look past Remo, but Remo blocked his vision. Palmer feinted left, then right, then jumped. Each time, Remo matched the move.

"If I had a suspicious nature, I'd say you didn't want me to see what's in there," Palmer said.

"The confidentiality of the trancee-medium relationship must be honored," Remo said weightily.

"Is that so?" Suddenly Palmer dropped to his stomach. Remo did the same. Then Palmer raised his head. "Aha!" he shouted before Remo could block his line of sight again.

At the sound, a troublesome body fell forward, crashing headfirst into the coffee table.

Palmer stood up, dusting himself off. "Those guys in there don't look too healthy," he said, giving Remo the once-over with his eyes.

"Hey. We don't ask for a certificate of health, okay? So what are you here about, anyway?"

Palmer pursed his lips, as if deciding whether or not to arrest Remo on the spot. Then his mouth relaxed, and his face formed into its normal ferocious scowl. "Ah, what the hell," he said. "It's been a lousy enough day. We came by to tell you about your car."

"Car?"

"The rental. It blew up, remember?"

"Oh, yeah." The car had been the last thing on Remo's mind. "What was wrong with it?"

"What do I look like, a mechanic?" Palmer said crankily. "It had an extra part. A bomb."

Out of the corner of his eye, Remo saw another body keeling over.

"Uh . . . that's fine."

"Palmer's face reddened. "Oh, it's fine, is it?"

"No. I mean, it's not fine," Remo stammered. "It's terrible. What's the world coming to? A damn shame, that's what it is. . . ."

Palmer checked his watch with a sigh. "Five o'clock, and I need this? Come on, Madame Zelda. You and your friend are going to the station." He reached an arm through the opening of the door.

Remo touched two fingers to Palmer's wrist and paralyzed it.

"Wha—"

Remo tapped the detective's throat. No further sound came out.

"Listen," Remo said. "I know this looks suspicious, but we can't explain anything except that we're on your side. You can believe us or not, but you can't take us in. Physically can't."

As the detective gaped at Remo in mute surprise, his arm stiffly outstretched, Remo said, "But I'll tell you what we know. One, somebody killed the lawyer named Weems. You probably already knew that, and you've probably guessed that it's got something to do with the Billy Martin murder. Two, we think Billy was part of a drug ring that uses kids as street pushers. The top guys in the ring aren't kids, though, and we're trying to find out who they are. But we're not going to find out anything if cops are always hanging around us, so we'd appreciate it if you'd get lost for a while."

Then he touched Palmer's throat to release the paralyzed muscles.

"Why, you—" the detective began. Remo tapped the muscles again, and Palmer fell into an angry silence.

"I guess you don't believe the part about not being able to arrest us," Remo said. Palmer narrowed his eyes. Remo reached out and manipulated a spot on the detective's collarbone that caused Palmer's eyes to widen in pain.

"Do you believe me now?"

Palmer nodded.

Remo released the man's collarbone and then his arm. "I'm sorry I had to do that," he said.

Palmer nodded again, then pointed to his mouth.

"But do you *really* believe?" Remo said, trying to imitate Peter Pan.

The detective rolled his eyes. Remo touched his throat.

"Ah. Ah," Palmer said, holding his hand to his throat experimentally. "How'd you do that?"

"It's not easy to explain," Remo said. He told Palmer about the drug arrest figures and the elusive connection between the cities of New York, New Orleans, Los Angeles, and Detroit.

Palmer mulled over the information in silence for a

few moments. "Who do you work for?" he asked finally.

Remo shook his head. "Sorry."

"Government?"

"Can't say."

"It's government," Palmer said with finality. "No hit man can do the kind of thing you just did." He turned to leave, then turned back. "Just do me a favor, okay?"

"Shoot."

"Let me in on your discoveries next time. Just so some innocent rookie don't decide to arrest you and end up in the funny farm."

"Will do," Remo said.

"And another thing. You better use a different name the next time you rent a car. That bomb was for you. Somebody's got you pegged."

"That's okay. We can take care of ourselves."

"Somehow," Palmer said, rubbing his throat, "that doesn't surprise me."

CHAPTER TEN

The following morning Remo put a call in to Smith from the hotel room and filled him in on the attempts on both his and Chiun's lives.

"Why an attempt on Chiun?" Smith asked.

"I've been thinking about that," Remo said. "I'm pretty sure it was meant to be an attempt on me. They were just unlucky enough to find Chiun instead."

"Any problem with the local police?"

"No. We seem to have stumbled into a fairly good working relationship with the detective who arrested the Martin kid."

"What kind of relationship?" Smith asked suspiciously.

"Umm . . ." Remo knew how Smith felt about outsiders knowing anything at all about CURE. "He thinks we're mediums," he said.

"The Detroit police use mediums to solve their cases?"

"Why not?" Remo said lightly. "Anyway, what did you get for me?"

"Some enlightening information. For one thing, Lorenzo Moorcock is the man's real name."

"You're kidding."

"I don't kid, Remo."

"Oh, yeah, I forgot for a second. Continue, please."

"He's a failed politician."

"Well, he's got good training for what he's doing now, that's for sure."

"He ran for city commissioner in Detroit a few years ago and lost, but the interesting part is where he got large transfusions of money for his campaign."

"All right, Smitty, I'll bite. Where?"

"He received large donations from Iranian groups, both legal and illegal."

"That explains why he was singing the praises of the Ayatollah in his sermon. What other kinds of friends does he have?"

"Well, since then he's started this modern-beliefs religion, and he's made close friends with some Mexican officials who visit Detroit regularly as some sort of Mexican trade delegation to observe how cars are built here. Apparently, they visit his church for services while they are here. The Mexicans come fairly frequently—several times a year."

"Iranians and Mexicans, that's an odd pair."

"Very odd. What do you plan to do now?"

"I'm not sure. I guess I'll have to keep a close eye on Moorcock for a while and also talk to the other man I asked you to check up on for me. What did you get on him?"

"Louis Sterling. He's been working at National Motors as long as Allan Martin had been. His son is fifteen. His name is Walter."

"I'll want to talk to him again too. He was involved in what looked like a drug sale the other night, so he looks like my best bet to get some information on this drug ring."

"Do you know where to find him?"

"I'm hoping that he went back home last night, but if he saw me at Moorcock's church, he might be hiding out. If that's the case, I'll just have to hunt him up."

"Well, do what you have to do, and keep me informed."

"Always, Smitty," Remo said. He was about to hang up when something occurred to him. "Smitty, when is the next Mexican trade delegation due?"

"Wait, I'll check with the computer." A few moments went by, and then Smith said, "Just by coincidence, they're due in town tomorrow."

"Bingo. Thanks, Smitty. I'll keep in touch."

When he hung up, Chiun looked at him expectantly, and he went over the conversation with Smith.

"This minister has some very strange friends," Chiun remarked.

"One of us ought to keep an eye on him," Remo said, "while the other one looks for Walter Sterling."

"I will watch the minister," Chiun said. "He interests me."

"Then I'll get out there and try to find the Sterling kid. He's the only lead we have on this drug ring, and maybe he can lead us to whoever's in charge."

"And that will be the person responsible for the killing of the children."

Remo closed his eyes and said, "Yes, Chiun."

As they got ready to leave, Remo said, "No matter what happens, we'll meet back here this evening. If I can't find the Sterling kid, I want to follow the good minister tomorrow when he meets his friends from the Mexican trade commission."

"If you find the boy—" Chiun began.

"I know," Remo said, "I'll be nice to him. I'll buy him a lollipop and ask him real nice to tell me who his source is."

Remo decided against saddling himself with another rental car and took a cab to the Sterling house. He didn't bother wondering how Chiun was going to get around, or how the Oriental would follow the minister without being spotted. He knew that if Chiun didn't want to be seen, he could be damned near invisible.

When he reached the Sterling house, there was no car in front or in the driveway, but then he hadn't expected Louis Sterling to be home. It was Walter he was after.

He rang the bell, hoping against hope that the kid himself would answer. When there was no immediate reply, he rang again, deciding he'd settle for the kid's mother. When no one answered the second ring, he put his hand on the doorknob, exerted just the right amount of pressure, and popped it open.

It only took a few moments for him to ascertain that the house was empty, and then he started his search. He was looking for a large stash of money or anything else that might help him. When he found what was obviously the kid's bedroom, he spent more time there than anywhere else and was rewarded. In the closet he found some loose floorboards and, prying them up, discovered what he was looking for. Not only did he find the cash, but there were some drugs hidden away as well. Still, there was nothing to tell where either had come from, so he left them there and replaced the floorboards.

He left the house and decided that he might as well go to the plant and talk to Louis Sterling, who might be able to tell him where his son was.

When he got to the plant, he received a pass from the same receptionist he had seen on his first visit and went looking for Sterling on the assembly line. When he didn't see him, he asked the foreman, Boffa, if he knew where he was.

"Did you check the lounge?"

"Yeah, he's not there."

"What about the locker room?"

"I don't know where it is."

Checking his watch, the foreman frowned and then said, "All right, come on, I'll show you."

Remo followed Boffa to the locker room, where they found Louis Sterling crouched down in front of his open locker.

"Lou—" Boffa began, but he stopped when he noticed something funny. Remo noticed also that Sterling wasn't crouched. He was slumped against the locker.

And dead.

"What the hell . . ." the foreman said.

Remo touched the man on the shoulder and leaned over him. In the middle of Sterling's chest was a gaping knife wound.

Remo left the plant in a hurry, not even stopping to drop off his badge. With Louis Sterling dead, Walter Sterling couldn't be that far behind. Obviously, Remo had gotten too close when he latched on to the Sterlings, and the intention now was to remove them before he could get anything out of them.

"Call the police and ask for Detective Palmer," Remo said, giving Boffa quick instructions. "Tell him I was here—that's Randisi—but I had to leave."

"Shouldn't you wait?"

"Louis Sterling is dead, and I think his son Walter is next on the list. Tell Palmer I'll get in touch with him when I can."

After that, he left the plant and hailed a cab. He wanted to go to the Church of Modern-day Beliefs and check in with Chiun. Maybe the Sterling kid was inside the church with Moorcock.

Remo was sure that no one had been able to spot Chiun for the simple reason that it had taken him fifteen minutes to spot him himself. The wily Oriental had simply taken up position in the shadows between the slats of the fence behind the alley where Remo had watched the drug deal go down.

"It took me awhile to see you," Remo said, joining Chiun behind the fence.

"I know," Chiun said. "I allotted you fifteen minutes to find me, and then showed myself."

"Right," Remo said. Chiun would never admit that Remo had spotted him on his own.

"Why are you here so soon?" Chiun asked.

"Things are starting to happen." He told Chiun what he had found in the Sterling house, and then what he found when he went to the plant. "The kid has to be next," he summed up.

"We must keep that from happening," Chiun said.

"That's why I'm here," Remo said. "You haven't seen any . . . children go into the church, have you?"

"No, none."

"Well, that doesn't mean he wasn't in there when you got here," Remo said. "How about Moorcock? Did you see him leave?"

"No."

"I think I'd better go in and have a talk with him. If he knows where the kid is, maybe I can convince him to tell me."

"I will come with you."

"I think it would be better if you stayed here. If Walter Sterling is in there, he might take off the back way when he sees me."

"Very well, but you must try your best to get the man to help us. It is vital that no more children die."

"For once, Chiun, I agree with you."

Remo left the cover of the broken fence and crossed the street to the church. When he entered, he found the place empty, and he was frankly surprised that the doors were not locked. As he started down the center aisle, a door in the front of the church opened, and Lorenzo Moorcock, minister and failed politician, came out.

"You have come back," he said. "To worship?"

"To ask for help."

"It is the same thing."

Remo stopped where he was and spoke to Moorcock from across the room. "I'm going to be very frank with you, Reverend."

"How refreshing."

"I'm looking for a boy named Walter Sterling. Do you know him?"

"He is a member of my flock, as is his family."

"His father isn't anymore," Remo said. "He's dead, and I think whoever killed him is out there looking for Walter right now to do the same to him."

"Why would anyone want to kill the boy?"

"Because he's involved with drugs, and he's become a liability to whoever he's working for."

Moorcock stared at Remo for a few seconds and then said, "How do I know that you don't simply want to arrest the boy for dealing drugs?"

"I'm not a policeman, Moorcock. I've told you that."

"Yes, you have, but I can't help but notice that you act very suspiciously like a policeman—"

"Moorcock, if you were any kind of a minister, you'd want to keep that boy from being killed—"

"How would you suggest I do that?"

"Tell me where he is."

"And if he shows up dead anyway, I would have

no recourse but to suspect you of having something to do with it."

"You've got a suspicious nature for a minister," Remo said. "Or maybe I should say, for an ex-politician."

Moorcock did not look surprised that Remo knew something about his past. "You are well informed," he said. "A policeman would be."

"What do I have to do to convince you?"

"Suppose I think about that question for a while and then get back to you," the minister suggested.

"Reverend, I wouldn't wait too long if I were you," Remo said. "And to make it easy, here's the number where I'm staying."

"That sounds like a threat."

"Take it any way you want."

Remo started for the exit, then turned to face the minister again. "Talk to the boy, Moorcock. Give him a chance to decide his own fate."

"I'll be in touch."

Remo left the church and walked directly across the street to where Chiun was watching.

"Did anyone leave the building?" he asked.

"No one," Chiun said. "I take it the minister was not very cooperative."

"He's a suspicious man," Remo said, "or he wants us to think he is."

"What does that mean?"

"He's more than he seems to be," Remo said. "Maybe tomorrow we'll find out, when the Mexicans arrive."

"And until then?"

"He's supposed to call me if he decides to cooperate. I think one of us should go back to the hotel and wait for that call."

"Do you really think it will come?"

"I don't think I want to take a chance that it will and we aren't there to answer."

"What have you in mind?"

"I think you should go back, Little Father. I want to try another way of bringing Walter Sterling to the surface."

"How?"

"I'm going to ask someone else for help."

"Detective Palmer?"

"I'll have to talk to him, yes," Remo said, "but even before I see Palmer, I want to go and see an old friend of mine—a pusher named Danny the Man."

"What makes you think he will help?"

"I'll ask him real nice, Chiun," Remo said. "You know how persuasive I can be."

CHAPTER ELEVEN

Danny the Man wasn't expecting company . . . again. This time the young lady was white, blond, and busty instead of willowy, and she was right in the middle of earning her "candy" when there was a knock at the door.

"Jesus!" Danny the Man said viciously.

"Mmmm?" the girl asked.

"Let me loose, Carla, I got to answer that."

"Mmm-mmm," the girl said, unwilling to give up when she was so close to earning her fix.

"Business before pleasure, Carla, honey," the black man said. He gave her an open-handed slap alongside her head and snapped, "Let me loose, dammit!"

The girl allowed him to slip away, and then pouted as he swung his legs to the floor, stood up, and put on his silk robe.

As he was heading for the door, the knocking became a pounding, and he wondered which of his customers was so hard up for a fix already. He was sure that business had been concluded for that particular day. Danny the Man knew his regular customers, and knew when they were due to fix, and that meant that whoever was knocking wasn't a customer.

Cops, he wondered, or . . . Naw, it couldn't be that crazy white dude again, could it?

He swung the door open and said, ''Aw, man . . .''

''Hello, Danny,'' Remo said, walking past the pusher into the apartment.

''Man, you can't be doing this to me all the time. My sex life is turning to shit.''

''Try getting some nice young lady to do it for love, Danny, and not for candy.''

''Thank you, Dear Abby,'' Danny said. He slammed the door shut and put his hands on his hips, facing Remo. ''What is it this time?''

''Before we start, why don't you keep your friend from walking out here naked. I'd hate to have to play that whole scene again.''

''And I can't afford to have you cure another one of my girls,'' Danny agreed. ''Wait a sec.''

Danny went into the bedroom, and Remo heard him exchange a few less than friendly words with a young lady. In a few moments the pusher was stepping back into the room, pulling the bedroom door shut behind him.

''You got anything on under that robe?''

''What the hell do you think I was doing when you barged in,'' Danny said, ''dressing for the policeman's ball?''

"Just see if you can keep the robe from falling open. I don't think I could take the excitement."

"Ha-ha. I'm dying laughing." He poured himself a drink. "You want one this time?"

"No."

Danny sat down on the couch, taking care not to allow his robe to gape open. "All right, man, lay it on me. What do you want?"

"I want your help finding somebody."

"Who?"

"A kid pusher named Walter Sterling."

Danny made a face and said, "Don't sound like the name of one of my people."

"He's not. He's white."

"A street pusher?"

"Yeah."

Danny shrugged and said, "I don't know him."

"That may be so, but that doesn't mean you can't help me find him."

"How do you propose I do that?"

"You've got street people of your own, Danny. Put the word out. One white boy can't be that hard to find in this neighborhood, right?"

"What makes you think he's hanging out here?"

Remo shrugged and said, "A hunch. If he's hiding out, he's hiding where he thinks no one will look for him."

"You want my people to find this kid for you," Danny said. "Is that all?"

"Not quite. The next part is tricky."

"I don't like tricks."

"You'll love it. It'll spice up your life."

"I hate it already."

"I want you to front for me in setting up a meeting with someone from this new drug operation."

"We've had meetings. Nothing ever gets done," Danny said. "The top man never comes."

"I don't want the top man. I just want somebody I can question."

"What makes you think that whoever they send will talk to you?" the pusher asked.

"I'm a real persuasive guy, Danny."

"Man, I'll bet you are too."

"What do you say?"

"I say maybe I ought to give you a try," Danny said, giving Remo an appraising look.

"You carrying your blade in that?"

"I wouldn't need my blade."

"Oh, yes, you would," Remo said, "and that would still give you next to no chance at all." They stared at each other in silence for several ticks of the clock, and then Remo said, "Believe me."

"That's the problem, man," Danny said. "I do."

"You'll set it up, then?"

"I'll give it a shot. Where do I get in touch with you when—and *if*—I do?"

Remo gave Danny the Man his hotel and his room number.

"Call me there. I'll be waiting for another call anyway, so someone will be there at all times."

"Got some other fool working for you too?"

"Working," Remo said. "But I don't think it's for me."

*   *   *

Remo's next stop was the police station, where Detective William Palmer was breathing fire.

"What the hell do you mean by leaving the scene of a homicide?" the detective demanded. "I could put you away for that and throw away the key. You know that, don't you?"

"I know. But you won't."

"And why not?" The detective placed his hands belligerently on his hips.

"Because I'm going to solve these murders for you."

"Is that a fact? You got some kind of crystal ball?"

"I'm just working on something, that's all."

Palmer stared at Remo, breathing hard through his nose, and then said, "What about the kid? Did you find him?"

"Not yet. That's one of the things I'm working on."

"And where's your friend?"

"He's back at the hotel, resting."

"Yeah," Palmer said. "If I killed six men, I'd need a rest too."

"What are you talking about?" Remo said casually.

"Six stiffs showed up in the parking lot behind your hotel this morning." The detective lit a cigarette. "Funny thing," he said through a jet of blue smoke.

"Every last one of them's a known killer with a record a mile long. And enough juvenile offenses to fill the side of a building."

"Do tell," Remo said.

"Don't get smart with me, Zorro. It don't matter

that they were scumbags. Detroit ain't no place for vigilantes, no matter who they work for." He stabbed his finger into Remo's chest. "You and the old geezer just better watch your ass, get it?"

"Look, you know I didn't have anything to do with killing Louis Sterling."

"Mister," Palmer said, "I don't know *nothing* about you. And that's the way I want to keep it."

"I know, and I appreciate it. You won't be sorry."

"Hell, I'm already sorry. Go on, get your butt out of here before I come to my senses."

"I'll be in touch."

"I can't wait."

Back at the hotel Chiun told Remo that the minister had not yet called, but that a man named Danny Lincoln had.

"That's Danny the Man, Chiun. What did he say?"

"He said that he had put the word out but had not yet been able to make that appointment you wanted. He will call you tomorrow."

"Well, I guess that means we can stop waiting for the phone to ring tonight."

"The child Walter Sterling is still out there, in danger," Chiun said.

"With a little luck, Chiun, that'll change tomorrow."

"Tomorrow you will follow the minister?"

"Yes, while you wait for Danny the Man to call. He's either going to find the kid for us or put us in contact with someone else involved with the drug selling. One way or the other we could wrap this thing up tomorrow."

"We will have to make sure that luck has nothing to do with it," Chiun said. "Only a white barbarian would trust success to luck. The welfare of the children of the world must not be left to chance."

"Right, Chiun."

"So tomorrow we will make sure that this matter comes to an end, and the killer of children will be punished."

"I'm with you, Chiun," Remo said.

"I hope that is not meant to be a source of encouragement to me."

CHAPTER TWELVE

Lorenzo Moorcock turned to Walter Sterling and said, "He wants to kill you, Walter."

"What makes you say that?" the kid asked.

"I can see it on his face, in his eyes. This Remo Randisi is a born killer. It is what he does."

The Reverend Moorcock had no idea just how right he was. "The best thing for you to do is stay right here until everything blows over, believe me."

"But my mother," Sterling said. "She'll be worried about me."

"Don't worry about your mother," Moorcock said. "I will tell her that you are all right."

They were in a small room on the second floor of the church, where Walter Sterling had been hiding since the first time Remo followed him. Now that Moorcock had told him that his father was dead, Walter was terrified that he was next.

"I will bring you something to eat later," Moorcock promised him. "For now, you had better rest."

"Thank you, Reverend," Sterling said, grabbing the man's arm. "Thank you."

"Not at all, my boy," Moorcock said, patting his hand. "After all, you are part of my flock."

Moorcock disengaged Sterling's hands from his arm and left the room. He took the steps down to the main floor but did not stop there. He went through another door and continued down until he reached the basement. A man was standing at the door as he entered the basement.

"How is it going?" Moorcock asked him.

"It's going fine."

"Will we be ready for our Mexican friends tomorrow?"

"More than ready. We'll be able to handle everything they bring us."

"Good," Moorcock said.

"What about the Sterling boy?" the man asked.

"He's all right where he is for now."

"I still think we should have killed him days ago when—"

"I'm aware of your opinion, Donald," Moorcock said, putting his hand on the man's shoulder. "You'll get your chance to kill him soon enough."

"You don't think I like killing, do you?" the man asked.

"No, Donald," Moorcock said, "I think you love it."

Both men laughed, and Moorcock went to look over his operation.

*   *   *

Lorenzo Moorcock had been a very unhappy man the day he lost the election for city commissioner of Detroit. But now, five years later, he couldn't have been happier about the outcome. If he had been successful in his political career, he wouldn't now be the proud owner of a wildly lucrative drug operation.

It had taken Moorcock time to set up his elaborate drug-cutting factory in the basement, after he had purchased the run-down church. But the church was a perfect cover, and once he had that set up, it was just a matter of rounding up the right people and the right contacts. Some of his old political affiliations had been helpful in that area, especially his Iranian friends.

Using juveniles as his street peddlers had been a stroke of pure genius. When they got arrested, it was only on juvenile charges, and they were soon out on the streets again. And when they got older, he simply moved them into another area of the operation.

It was all perfect, right down to the way the drugs were brought into the country and placed in his hands. For that, he used not only the Iranians but also the Mexicans.

In the eighteen months that his operation had been running, no one had ever come close to impeding it . . . until now. The American and the Oriental were becoming dangerous and would have to be dealt with. He wouldn't want his Mexican friends to find out about them and get nervous. Removing them would have to be handled carefully because the Mexicans would be in town tomorrow. For once Moorcock admitted to himself that he may have made a mistake. He should have listened to Donald and let him kill the pair sooner.

Of course, he hadn't realized how difficult they'd be to kill. The American had somehow scared away the kids who had been sent to kill him on the street, and then he'd managed somehow to get back to the hotel in time to save the old man.

This time he'd send seasoned men after them and get the job done right.

While he was inspecting the cutting operation to make sure everything was in order, Donald came up next to him with a message.

"From whom?" Moorcock asked.

"Danny the Man Lincoln."

"The nigger dealer?"

"That's the guy."

"What does he want?"

"He wants a meeting."

"With me?"

"Actually, the word is he just wants to meet with someone from our operation."

"For what purpose?"

"I don't know."

"Perhaps he wants to join us.

"God knows he can't beat us."

"Please," the minister said, "we do not speak of God here. He is not part of our modern beliefs."

"Right, right," Donald said, wondering how serious Moorcock was.

"All right, Donald," Moorcock said. "Set it up.

Arrange the meeting with Mr. Danny the Man. Who knows? Maybe he could be useful to us.''

''When should I set it up for?''

''Tomorrow night, I think. I'll want you with me when we meet with the Mexicans.''

''You'll want me with—uh, you mean I'm going to meet with him?''

''Who else would I send, Donald?'' Moorcock asked. ''You are my right-hand man.''

''Yes, sir.''

''Everything looks all right here, Donald. I'll be upstairs if you need me.''

''Yes, sir.''

Moorcock took one last glance around and then went upstairs to prepare for evening services.

Donald Wagner didn't like the idea of having to meet with Danny the Man. He didn't like blacks, and in fact it made him very nervous to work in the ghetto. Of course, he'd never let Moorcock know that. He hid his fear through viciousness—and through killing. Killing for the sake of killing made him feel like a man. He wouldn't have minded meeting Danny the Man to kill him, but to talk business with him— that was another matter.

Still, he worked for Moorcock, and everything the ''minister'' had done up to this point had been successful. The man was strange and probably more than a little crazy, but there was no doubt that he was a genius.

If Lorenzo Moorcock wanted him to meet with Danny the Man, that's what he would do.

After all, what harm could it do?

* * *

When the phone rang, Danny the Man cursed aloud. The young lady beneath him was just lifting her hips in anticipation when he withdrew, rolled over, and answered the phone.

"This better be *real* good," he said.

"Is this Danny the Man?"

"Yeah. Who's this?"

"I'm calling to arrange a meeting."

"Am I supposed to know what that means?"

"I'm sure you do. This is a meeting that you've been asking for."

He should have known. If it wasn't that white bastard himself—with his usual timing—it would be his business that the call was about.

"All right," Danny said. "When?"

"Tomorrow evening, after dark. Let's make it nine o'clock," the man's voice said.

"Are you white?" Danny asked.

"What?" the man asked, puzzled.

"You sound white. Are you?"

"Of course I am. What the hell does that have to do with anything?"

"I was just wondering if you wouldn't feel at a disadvantage meeting a black man after dark."

He got great satisfaction from the flustered sound of the man's voice as he recited where the meeting would be. Since Danny had no intention of being there, he readily agreed to the meeting place.

"Anything else?" he asked then.

"No," the man's voice said petulantly, "there's nothing else. Just be there."

"I will if you will," Danny said. For a moment he thought the man would answer, but then the line went dead.

The girl on the bed said, "Jesus Christ, Danny, I was almost there."

Her hands reached out for him, and he crawled back on top of her, saying, "The least you could have done for me, bitch, was keep your finger in my place."

In Mexico City three Iranian diplomats were meeting with three Mexican officials who would be flying to the United States the following morning.

Rafael Cintron was the leader of the Mexicans, the one who had recruited the other two, Antonio Jiminez and Pablo Santoro.

"This will be the largest shipment we have ever carried, Rafael," Jiminez said. "Should we not take more precautions?"

"What would you suggest we do, my friend?" Cintron asked. "Take an armed guard? No, our methods work so well because they are simple. Just three Mexican officials carrying their diplomatic pouches. That is what makes the plan so beautiful."

"*Si*, I know that—"

"Well, if you know that, then stop worrying."

There was a knock on the hotel-room door, signaling the arrival of the merchandise.

"Answer the door, Pablo."

Santoro opened the door, and the three Iranian diplomats entered, one of them carrying a black attaché case. They all knew what was in the case.

Heroin with a street value of over three million dollars.

The Iranians stayed only long enough for the merchandise to change hands. Names were not even exchanged. The mere fact that they were all in that one place at the same time meant that it was right.

The handoff was made, and the H was on its way to the United States of America—or, to be more specific, the city of Detroit.

CHAPTER THIRTEEN

The following morning Remo was gone by the time the call came in from Danny the Man.

"Are you his friend?" Danny asked when Chiun explained that Remo wasn't there.

"I am his . . . companion," Chiun said.

"Well, tell him that the meeting has been set up, like he asked me. I'll give you the place. Get something to write it down with."

"You may proceed," Chiun said.

Danny the Man recited the address, then added, "Your pal better wear some blackface if he hopes to pass as a black man, even after dark. "They're expecting me, so if they see a white face, they might start shooting first."

"I will tell him. I'm sure he will be touched by your concern."

"And tell him that if he needs any more favors, he should try somebody else for a change. I'd like at least one night of uninterrupted pleasure."

129

"I will tell him."

"Hey, you white? You don't talk like no white man."

Chiun hung up the phone and said, "Perish the thought."

Remo was standing across the street from the Church of Modern-day Beliefs, in a doorway from which he couldn't be seen. He was expecting Moorcock to leave the building fairly soon in order to meet the incoming Mexican delegation, but was surprised when a long black limo pulled up in front of the church and three men who were obviously Mexican stepped out. One of them, carrying a dark attaché case, said something to the driver, who then left. The three men entered the church.

"Welcome, my friends," Lorenzo Moorcock said. "I'm glad to see you again."

"Señor Moorcock," Rafael Cintron said, accepting the minister's outstretched hand. The Mexicans not only accepted Moorcock as their business partner, but as a minister as well. "We are honored to be in your house of worship."

Cintron realized that Moorcock's religion forbade the mention of God, and while it puzzled him, he respected it as he was a deeply religious man himself. No matter how odd another man's beliefs were, they were to be respected.

"We can go downstairs, where I will serve you refreshments, and then we can get on about our business."

"*Gracias.*"

As Moorcock led the Mexicans to the basement steps, they noticed two men descending from steps above. Moorcock saw their interest and said, "Just two of my flock. Please, gentlemen, be my guests downstairs."

"*Gracias,*" Cintron said again, and down they went.

One of the two men leaving the church by the rear door was Jim Burger, who was acting on orders from Donald Wagner. He was to escort the second man to a nice, quiet place . . . and then kill him.

The second "man" was Walter Sterling.

From across the street, Remo could watch not only the front entrance but the side as well. Now as he watched, he saw two people leave that way. The first he didn't recognize, but the second he did. It was the Sterling kid. He watched as the first man led Walter Sterling to a car. When the kid saw three other men in the car, he balked, but they forced him into the car, and then it drove away.

Remo broke from his doorway and ran across the street. He was in time to use his ultra-keen hearing to listen to what was being said in the car.

"Where to?" one man said.

"The junkyard," another man said. "The big one on Maple."

As the car drove away, Remo knew he had a choice to make. He could stay and watch the church, waiting for Moorcock or his guests to come out, or he could go after the men in the car and save Walter Sterling's life.

Knowing that Chiun would never forgive him if the Sterling kid got killed, he decided to go after the car. If the Mexicans had come to the church to meet Moorcock, then it was almost a certainty that Moorcock would not leave the church when his guests did.

Remo started after the car, and although he knew he could catch it, even on foot, he decided against it. Instead, he used his superior speed to arrive at the Maple junkyard ahead of them.

When he arrived, he saw that there were already three men there. He didn't know if they simply worked there or if they were part of the drug gang, so he left them alone for the moment. He vaulted the fence and waited among the countless car wrecks for the opportunity to save one of Chiun's children.

The car arrived about ten minutes after Remo had. The four men who were in it accompanied Walter Sterling into the Detroit Auto Cemetery.

"What are we supposed to do with him?" one of the three men who worked in the junkyard asked.

"We have to find him a nice resting place," Burger replied. "The boss's orders."

"I don't understand," Sterling said. "Did you men kill my father? We were doing our part."

"We're just removing you, sonny, before you can do more than your part," Burger said.

The three junkyard employees remained at the entrance to see that the others wouldn't be disturbed.

"Take him in the back," one of them said. "There's a nice Rolls-Royce there almost still in one piece."

The four men walked toward the rear of the yard

with the Sterling boy between them, still blubbering about how he didn't understand why they were doing this.

"Boss's orders, boy," Burger finally said. "Nothing personal."

"Donald?" the boy asked. "Did he tell you to kill me?"

"I'm talking about the big boss, sonny. Now keep quiet and try to die like a man."

"Oh, Jesus—" Sterling shouted, but his cry was cut off as a small Volkswagen suddenly flew off the top of a pile of cars and headed right for the group.

"Look out!" Burger screamed, and the five of them scattered. The Volkswagen landed squarely in the center of the space they had previously occupied.

"What the hell was that?" one of the other men yelled.

"Somebody threw a car at us," another man said.

"That ain't possible," Burger shouted at them. "Don't go crazy. A car just fell from the top, that's all. Where's the boy?"

"The boy—" the others said, and they all started looking around them, but the boy was nowhere to be seen.

"Dammit!" Burger shouted. "Find him."

As they gathered into a group again, another car came flying at them, this time a Pinto.

"Christ, look out!"

"Now tell me somebody ain't throwing cars at us," one of the men told Burger.

"This is crazy—" Burger started to say, but he shut his mouth as he dodged a Plymouth Duster.

"Christ almighty, they're getting bigger!" he shouted.

"I'm getting out of here before a fuckin' Caddy comes flying at us!" one of the others yelled.

"Wait, what about the kid?" Burger said.

"As far as I'm concerned," the other man said, "he's dead. Right, men?"

The others all agreed. Burger was about to argue, but when a Buick Electra came flying toward them, he simply nodded and followed the other men.

As the four men ran out the front way, one of the others yelled, "Did you do it?"

"It's done, it's done!" they shouted back, and kept on going.

"What's the matter with them?" one of the three said. "They act like something tried to bite them.

Remo dropped Walter Sterling over the rear fence of the yard and then joined him.

"How'd you get rid of them?" Sterling asked. "I couldn't see anything after you put me in that car and told me to keep my head down."

"I just scared them a little, that's all, Walter. Come on, let's get going."

"Where?"

"We're going to my hotel. There's someone there I think you'll enjoy meeting."

"Wait—"

"What is it?"

"The minister said you wanted to kill me."

"Well, he was wrong," Remo said, "as you can see. If I wanted you dead, boy, you'd be dead."

"I—I guess so."

"Come on. We'll talk at the hotel."

For the benefit of the boy, Remo hailed a cab and had it take them back to the hotel. As they entered the hotel room, Walter Sterling stared at Chiun and asked, "Who's that?"

"That's Chiun," Remo said. "He's my—"

"—companion," Chiun finished.

"He's also the main reason you're alive," Remo said. "Chiun, this is Walter Sterling."

"We are sorry about your father, child," Chiun said.

"I still don't understand what's going on," the boy said shakily.

"Well, let us tell you what we know," Remo said, "and then you can fill us in if you're satisfied."

"A-all right," the boy said, sitting on the couch.

"Now, we've figured out that you're selling drugs and that there are other kids out there doing the same . . . like Billy Martin."

Sterling didn't reply.

"The Martins had a large stash of cash, and so do you," Remo said, and that startled the boy.

"How did—"

"I found it. Don't worry, I left it where it was."

"That's for my mother, now that my father's gone."

"Your father—now, that puzzles me. Did he know that you were selling drugs?"

"Yeah, he did," the kid said. Then he gave Remo and Chiun a defiant look and said, "We were just trying to make some extra money, that's all."

"What was your father's part?"

"He used his position at the plant to ship the drugs to other cities."

"So that's it," Remo said. "That's why kids whose fathers work at the plant were recruited. You, Martin . . . Were there others?"

"I don't know. We were never really told more than we needed to know."

"That is wise," Chiun said.

"Hell, that means you don't know anything beyond your own personal duties."

"That's right."

"Well, if I knew that, I would have saved one of those guys at the yard for questioning."

"As usual, you were sloppy," Chiun said, "but lucky for you your friend called."

"Danny the Man?"

"Yes. He said that your meeting has been set up," Chiun said, and then proceeded to recite the location.

"Do you know where that is?" Remo asked Sterling.

"Yes."

"Good, you can give me directions."

"Who are you meeting?" Sterling asked.

"Damned if I know," Remo said. "Who's in charge of this operation as far as you know?"

"A man named Donald Wagner always gave me my instructions," Walter Sterling said. "As far as I know, he's the boss."

"Not from what the men in the junk yard said," Remo recalled. "One of them told you that it was the 'big boss' who wanted you out of the way."

"I don't know who that is."

"I don't, either—at least, not for sure," Remo said, "but hopefully I'll be meeting someone tonight who will know."

"Maybe he won't tell you."

"Yes," Chiun said, "he will tell. He will have no choice."

"Have you been hiding at the church all this time?" Remo asked.

"Yes. The minister has been taking care of me."

"What do you know about him?"

The boy shrugged and said, "Just that he's a minister of some new religion. I don't exactly believe what he preaches, but he was helping me."

"Out of the goodness of his heart," Remo said.

"I suppose. What are you going to do now?"

"We'll wait," Remo said. "You give me the directions to my meeting, and then we'll wait until dark. You'll stay here with Chiun—"

"I'll go with you. I can show you how to get there better than I can tell you."

"I will go also," Chiun said. "I think this whole business is about to come to an end, and I intend to be there when it does."

"All right," Remo said.

"Besides," Chiun said, "I have to make sure that this child remains alive. He is my responsibility now."

"Whatever you say, Chiun. He's all yours."

Donald Wagner was gearing up for what he thought was a meeting with Danny the Man Lincoln. He inserted a .38 into his shoulder holster and then turned to face the five men he was taking with him.

"You're all armed?" he asked.

The men nodded. These were experienced men in their late twenties or early thirties. Wagner was not taking any chances by bringing kids along to back him up. Who knew what that nigger was planning for him?

"All right, we've picked an empty warehouse for this meeting, and you five will get there first. I want you all to be so well hidden on the catwalk that even I can't find you. But if something breaks, I want to see your ugly faces in a split second. Don't make me wonder where you are."

All five men nodded. He knew he could count on them because, unlike the majority of people involved in Moorcock's operation, they were pros.

He would feel better having them with him. What could go wrong with that many men to back him up?

Lorenzo Moorcock showed his Mexican guests out to the street, where their limousine was waiting to take them to their hotel. They would stay there for three days, during which time they would tour some of the automotive factories, and then they'd return to Mexico City. He wouldn't see them—or others like them—until the next shipment was due.

Reentering the church, Moorcock was excited. This was the largest and finest-quality shipment they'd ever had. He could cut it countless times, doubling or even tripling its normal worth.

As he approached the door to the basement, it

opened, and Donald Wagner stepped out, followed by five other men.

"Time for the meeting?" Moorcock asked.

"Yes."

"It should be interesting," the minister said, "but don't take too long. We have to discuss how to dispose of those two meddlers."

"We'll be back soon," Wagner said, with more confidence than he was feeling.

"Be careful," Moorcock warned. "We're on top of the biggest score we've ever had, and we can't take a chance of ruining it now. If there is even a hint that Mr. Lincoln is setting us up for something, get rid of him."

"That," Wagner said, patting his .38, "would be a pleasure."

CHAPTER FOURTEEN

"That's it," Walter Sterling said.

"Do you know anything about it?" Remo asked.

"As a matter of fact, I do," Walter Sterling said. "It's been empty since I was a kid. We used to play there—me and all my friends."

"Good. What's the best way of getting in there without being seen?" Remo asked.

"Over the top. We used to play on the roof."

"Then we'll go that way."

Remo knew that he and Chiun could have gone right through the front door without being seen, but they couldn't do that with Walter around. This way, all of them could enter the warehouse unnoticed.

"What's the best way to get up there?"

"The next building. Come on."

Walter took them up the steps to the roof of the building next door and then seemed disappointed.

"What's wrong?" Remo asked.

141

"Well, there used to be this big wooden beam that went from this roof to the roof of the warehouse." He looked around. 'It's not here.''

There were at least ten feet separating the two rooftops. Walter said, "We'll never get over there now.''

"Of course we will," Chiun said. "There is a plank on the other roof that you can use to get across.''

"Yes, but it's on the other roof," Walter said. As he spoke, he turned to face Chiun and did not see Remo easily leap to the roof of the warehouse. Nor did he see Remo pick up the plank and leap back with it. When he turned, the plank was there, in place, bridging the gap between rooftops.

"How did you do that?" he asked, staring at Remo in awe.

"That doesn't matter. Come on, let's get across.''

"Uh—''

"What's the matter?''

"This plank is about half the width of that old beam.''

"That doesn't matter," Remo said. "Chiun will take you across.''

With that, Remo walked across the plank as if it were the width of a city block.

"I can't—" Walter started to say, but Chiun cut him off.

"You can," the old man said. "Come, I'll go with you.''

Chiun got up on the plank and put his hand out to the boy. Walter took the hand and stepped up onto the plank.

"Don't look down, right?" he asked.

"Look at the plank," Chiun said. "How wide is it?"

"About six inches."

"Keep your eyes on it. Watch it grow. How wide is it now?" Chiun asked.

Walter Sterling stared in wonderment as the plank appeared to widen. "It's at least eight—no, nine inches wide now."

"You tell me when it's wide enough for you to walk on," Chiun said, "and we'll go."

Walter kept watching the plank, and it seemed to keep widening—to twelve inches, fifteen inches, a foot and a half . . .

"All right," he said, "let's go. We can't keep Remo waiting forever."

With Chiun walking ahead of him, Walter negotiated the length of the plank flawlessly, until he was standing on the roof of the warehouse.

"Sorry it took us so long," he said to Remo.

"What are you talking about?" Remo asked. "You came over right after I did. Come on, let's get moving."

"This way," Walter said, and led them to a large, heavy metal door. "It's locked."

"Stand back," Remo said.

"That door is inches thick," Walter said to Chiun. "We'll never get it open."

"Let's go," Remo said.

Walter turned to look at him and found that the door was already open. "How did you do that?"

Before Remo could answer, Chiun said, "You will have to learn to stop asking that question."

"Let's go down," Remo said.

Inside the stairway it was pitch black, as it now was outside as well.

"How are we going to see—" Walter began, but Chiun nudged him into silence.

The stairwell let out onto a catwalk, one of many crisscrossing the upper portion of the warehouse.

"Do you see them?" Remo asked.

"See who?" Walter asked.

"Of course I see them," Chiun said.

"See who?" Walter whispered.

"Five," Remo said, "all up here."

"Who?"

"Quiet!" Chiun hissed. "I will take the two nearest," he said to Remo, "you the other three."

They both looked down at the floor below and saw nothing.

"Whoever arranged the meeting hasn't shown up yet. We can get this done before he does," Remo said.

"What do I do?" Walter asked.

"Put your hand out in front of your face," Chiun said. Walter did so. "What do you see?"

"Nothing."

"Does that answer your question?" Remo asked.

Walter dropped his hand, and Chiun said, "Do not move until we get back."

"All right."

They were there, and then suddenly they weren't. Remo and Chiun simply blended into the darkness and were gone.

*   *   *

Soundlessly, Remo moved up behind the first man and pressed his finger into his back. "Don't make a sound," he said over the man's shoulder.

"Wha—" Jim Burger said.

"Take it easy."

"Okay, okay, just don't shoot, huh, buddy?"

"Shoot? What are you talking about?" Remo asked, jabbing his finger harder against the man's back. "It's just my finger."

"Hey, buddy, don't try to con me, all right?" the man said. "I know steel when I feel it."

"What are you doing here?"

"Waiting."

"Who are you supposed to kill?"

"Huh? Kill? What are you—"

"Don't try to con *me,* buddy," Remo said, jabbing the man hard. "You're not here to talk."

"Look, pal, I'm not alone."

"I know that. After I take care of you, I'll take care of your friends."

"You won't shoot," the man said with a sudden surge of confidence. "The others would be all over you if you did."

"You're right, I won't shoot," Remo said, "but you're going to be just as dead."

Remo forced his finger forward through the fabric of the man's clothing, where it pierced his skin like the blade of a knife. The man grunted and then slumped back against Remo, who lowered him to the floor of the catwalk.

He eliminated the other two men in similar fashion, leaving all three so that their blood seeped through the grilled floor of the catwalk and dropped down to the warehouse floor below.

When Remo returned to where they had left Walter Sterling, Chiun was already waiting, shaking his head.

"Sloppy technique," he said.

"What happened?" Walter asked.

"I thought it would be a nice touch," Remo said.

"Like the dripping of three faucets," Chiun said. "The sound is offensive to me."

"You have no imagination, Chiun."

Chiun was about to answer when there was a faint sound below. Only he and Remo heard it.

"What did you—" Walter started, but both Remo and Chiun silenced him, and the boy lapsed into an exasperated silence he swore not to break.

They all listened intently, and finally Walter realized what had happened. Someone had entered the warehouse by more conventional means than they had—the front entrance.

Remo and Chiun decided to let the man stew awhile.

Wagner entered the warehouse confidently, certain that all five of his men had him in their sights to protect him. He wondered if the black dealer had arrived yet.

He knew the warehouse pretty well, and he knew where the main switches were. He found them and threw the switch for the lights for the lower half of the warehouse. The upper portion was still swathed in darkness, which was fine by him. That would make it easy for his men to remain unseen.

Checking his watch, he saw that it was ten minutes past the time of the meeting. Where was that black bastard, anyway?

He started to wander around the floor, wondering what Moorcock would think about filling this place with drugs. How much would a warehouse full of H be worth, anyway? Billions?

As he was walking, he suddenly slipped on something slick and almost fell. Cursing, he looked down at his shoe and found something red staining the bottom. He looked behind him and saw that he had stepped into a puddle of blood. As he watched, another drop fell, and then another and another. He could actually *hear* them. Suddenly, he became aware of similar sounds coming from other areas. He found two other puddles of blood, also leaking from the catwalk.

"What the hell—"

"Effective, don't you think?" a voice behind him asked.

He turned so quickly that he stepped into a blood puddle and fell on his behind. From the floor he stared up at the man looking down at him—a white man with dark hair.

"Who the hell are you? Where'd you come from?"

"I came from up there," Remo said, pointing up. "And I think you already know who I am."

"Y-you're the guy—"

"Right, I'm the guy."

"Where's the . . . the black guy? The dealer? Where's Danny the Man?"

"Speaking from past experience, he's probably home making some little lovely earn her candy."

"What—I was supposed to meet him here."

"Alone, right?"

"Of course."

"Then you don't know anything about the five dead men on the catwalk?"

"Five men on the catwalk?" Wagner said. "I told some of them—wait a minute. Five *dead* men up on the catwalk?"

"Either that, or they've got really bad bloody noses," Remo said, looking down at the widening puddle of blood.

"Uh," Wagner said, getting slowly to his feet, "uh, no, I don't know anything about—"

"All right, let's forget about the dead men," Remo said.

"Good. I'll just be going—"

"You came here to meet someone, my friend," Remo said, "and that someone is me."

"You?"

"Yeah, we've got some things to talk about."

"Like what?"

"Like drugs."

"I don't know nothing about drugs."

"And I don't know anything about putting out a newspaper," Remo said, "but I used to sell them when I was a kid."

"Look, pal," Wagner said. "I'm leaving, and there's nothing you can do to stop me."

"Wanna bet?"

Wagner suddenly remembered that he had a .38

under his left arm and pulled it out. "Move out of my way," he said.

"Sorry."

"You're going to be even sorrier," Wagner said, and he pulled the trigger.

The gun went off with a deafening blast, but the man was still standing there.

He *couldn't* have missed.

"Try it again," the man suggested.

Wagner pulled the trigger again, and the only thing that happened was that the man was suddenly closer to him instead of falling down dead.

"That's impossible."

"I'd like to let you keep trying until you get it right, but we really don't have time for that," Remo said. He closed the distance between himself and the man, took the gun away, and twisted it like a pretzel.

"Here," he said, giving it back. "Let's talk."

"What do you want to know?"

"I want you to confirm a suspicion I have that Lorenzo Moorcock is the man behind this whole kiddie drug system. Am I right?"

"This could get me killed."

"Would you like to go up on the catwalk?"

"No!"

"I'm sure your friends would love to have you join them."

"That's okay," Wagner said, wishing that the damned nigger had shown up instead of this dude.

"Then tell me about Moorcock."

"He set up the whole operation. He used his political contacts to get it started."

"Where do the drugs come from?"

"Iran."

"Why Iran?"

"Well, he had plenty of Iranian supporters when he was in politics. The Iranians feel they're contributing to the downfall of the United States by supplying Moorcock with the drugs."

"But the drugs are brought in by Mexicans, isn't that so?"

"Yeah, but see, the Iranians fly to Mexico City, where they turn the stuff over to some Mexican diplomats, then the diplomats fly here to Detroit to see how cars are made."

"But they also stop at the Church of Modern-day Beliefs."

"Right, and they drop the stuff off there."

Wagner seemed to be warming to his subject. He was really quite impressed with Moorcock's operation. And if talking about it would keep him alive, it was fine with him.

"Where is the stuff processed?"

"We step on it right there, in the basement. We got a regular factory down there."

"And then it's doled out to the kids to sell on the streets, right?"

"Yeah, right."

"Kids like Billy Martin and Walter Sterling?"

"Yeah, them and others."

"By 'others', you mean kids whose fathers work in automobile factories?"

"Just some of them. We don't need too many."

"What's their end of it?"

"That's the beautiful part," Wagner said. "They hide the stuff in the fender wells of the cars, and then somebody at the other end picks it up. It works like a charm."

"So what went wrong?"

"Wrong?"

"Why did Billy Martin kill his parents?"

"That was the kid's own doing," Wagner said. "He said his father was starting to get nervous about the drug money and was gonna talk to the cops."

"So why'd he kill his mother too?"

Wagner shrugged and said, "Maybe she woke up at the wrong time, or maybe the old man confided in her. Hell, maybe the kid just wanted to use the opportunity to get rid of both of them at one time."

"And then what happened to him?"

"Well, when he got caught, we figured he'd talk his head off to help himself, so Moorcock gave the order to have him killed."

"After he was bailed out."

"Right. I had one of my boys call that lawyer and make the arrangements to get him out, and then a few of the boys took care of him."

"Who blew up my car?"

Wagner fidgeted on that one. "Well, I went to the rental office and got your name and your hotel and then sent in one of the men to plant the explosive."

"One of the men up on the catwalk?"

Wagner looked up nervously and said, "Yeah, a guy named Jim Burger."

"Good," Remo said. "I'd hate to leave that little bit of business unfinished."

"Can I go now?"

"No, not just yet, my friend. Shipping the drugs in the cars couldn't be going on at the plant without somebody in authority being in on it. Who is it?"

Wagner frowned and said, "All we needed was the foreman on the assembly line, and we bought him dirt cheap. They don't pay their workers all that much."

"Boffa."

"Right."

"Then he must have killed Louis Sterling."

"Right again."

A cool customer, that foreman, Remo thought. He must have just killed Sterling and then calmly shown Remo where the body was.

"And that's it?" Remo asked. "That's all you can tell me?"

"What else do you want to know?"

"Who makes the pickups at the other end of the car shipments?" Remo asked.

"That I don't know," Wagner said. "I only know the Detroit end of the business. Moorcock is the only one who knows the whole operation."

"Is that so?"

The cold look in the man's dark eyes sent a chill through Wagner's body, and he knew that he'd just signed his own death warrant unless he could talk his way out of it. "Of course, I could always find out for you," he said quickly. "I could go back to the church and—"

"Forget it, pal."

"No, really, I wouldn't mind—" Wagner stammered, but he could see that it was too late.

"I think it's time for you to join your friends."

"Up on the catwalk?"

"No," Remo said, reaching out for the man's throat. "In hell."

Chiun took Walter Sterling out the way they had come and met Remo in front of the warehouse.

"What about all those men?" Walter asked.

"They won't be coming out," Remo said.

"You killed them all?"

"They would have tried to kill us," Chiun said. "Do not feel sorry for them."

"What are we gonna do now? Go to the police?"

"Not yet," Remo said. "We're going to pay a visit to Mr. Moorcock, and then tomorrow we'll go to the plant and take care of the man who killed your father."

"You know who killed my father?"

"I do."

"Tell me."

"I'll show you . . . tomorrow, Walter."

They grabbed a cab and took it back to the hotel, where they put Walter Sterling to sleep on the couch.

"Want to go to church?" Remo asked.

"I have a suggestion," Chiun said.

"Let me have it if it's clean."

"Let us wait until morning before we go to the church."

"But that would give Moorcock time to get his shipment to the National Motors factory."

"Correct. We will take care of the factory under the church and then call the police to meet us at National Motors. By the time they arrive, we will have taken care of that too, and we will also have drugs to prove that we stopped a drug shipment."

"I like that," Remo said.

"It will be your job to stay in touch with Detective Palmer."

"Palmer? What for?"

Chiun made a face. "Someone must clean up," he said.

"Hasn't Donald returned yet?" Moorcock asked the man who was standing by the basement door.

"No, sir."

"Has he called?"

"No, sir."

"Donald is supposed to take the shipment over to Boffa at the plant in the morning."

"I can do that, sir. Or one of the others."

"It's Donald's job," Moorcock said with a worried frown. "Something's gone wrong with his meeting with that black dealer. Did he say where the meeting was to take place?"

The other man looked confused because he assumed that Moorcock would know that, and said, "Uh, no, sir, he didn't tell me."

"I suppose I should have paid more attention. . . . All right, Samuel, I guess if Donald doesn't return, you will have to make the trip to the plant."

"Yes, sir, I will."

"And if Donald doesn't return by tomorrow, I

think that some of our men will have to pay a visit to Danny Lincoln and find out why. If he has betrayed us, someone will have to make him pay.''

"I'd be happy to do it," the man said.

"And if tragedy has befallen Donald, I will need a good man to take his place."

"Yes, sir!"

"Perhaps you would be able to help me find one, Samuel. We will discuss it," Moorcock said, and then started upstairs.

If Samuel hadn't known from personal experience that the minister had no sense of humor, he would have thought that Moorcock was putting him on.

He wished he were.

Upstairs, Moorcock started making plans to abandon the operation and get away with as much cash as he could. Something had gone wrong, of that he was sure, and it was obviously time to regroup. He could set up operations in another city easily enough, utilizing his contacts once again. This was by no means the end, but it was the end in Detroit. There were a lot of men in his employ, however, who were waiting for their payoff, and he was hoping that he could get away before any of them caught on.

So the decision was made. Tomorrow was his last day in Detroit.

Before turning in for the night, Remo and Chiun briefly went over their plans for the following day.

The next day was Friday, and according to what Walter Sterling had told them, on Friday the Church of Modern-day Beliefs held services in the morning and in the evening.

"The church will be full of people tomorrow morning, then," Chiun said.

"We could wait until the afternoon," Remo said.

"Then we run the risk of not being able to stop the shipment from leaving the automobile factory."

"That's right," Remo said.

"Then we will just have to stay with our original plan."

"Hit the church in the morning, and the plant in the afternoon," Remo said.

"Yes. We will have to try to make sure that no innocent people are hurt at the church—"

"—especially children," Remo finished before Chiun could.

CHAPTER FIFTEEN

Remo, Chiun, and Walter stood across the street from Moorcock's church as the Friday morning worshipers filed in.

"I don't understand the appeal of Moorcock's new religion," Remo said to Walter.

"My mother always said that it was an alternative," Walter said.

"And your father?"

Walter grinned and said, "My father always said it was a bunch of shit. Boy, if he only knew that we were really working for the minister. He was right, the religion shit was just a bunch of shit."

"Maybe not," Remo said. "I saw people dropping money in those urns he calls collection plates. I think maybe that's how he first financed his drug deals. From the looks of his church, he sure never used the money to make improvements."

"He said that the money would not be spent on commercial things but on intangibles."

"What was that supposed to mean?"

Walter shrugged and said, "Nobody ever asked him."

"He's got a mesmerizing manner, all right," Remo said. "His voice, his eyes—he's probably able to get people to listen to whatever he says, without question."

"People are sheep," Chiun said.

"He knows how to play to people, that's all. That's what every fire-and-brimstone preacher has always been able to do."

"You sound like you admire him," Walter said.

"Not at all, Walter. I just recognize what he is."

"If he had been satisfied with being a minister, none of this would be necessary," Chiun said, "but he used his ability to influence people to go too far. He has caused the death of children such as yourself, and he must be punished."

"I'm not a child."

"Believe me, kid," Remo said, "to Chiun you're a child."

The last person seemed to have entered the church, and they were about to step from cover to cross the street when Walter Sterling pulled them back.

"Oh, no!" he said.

"What's the matter?" Remo asked.

"That woman walking down the block toward the church," the kid said.

"What about her?" Remo asked.

"It's my mother."

"Your mother?"

"If she goes in—I didn't know she attended Friday services. What you and Chiun are planning . . .''

"Let's see if she goes in," Remo said.

The three of them watched the woman as she made her way down the street toward the church. When she reached the front steps, she ascended them without hesitation and entered the building.

"Damn!" Walter said.

"Take it easy—" Remo said.

"You can't do it, not now," Walter said. "I don't know exactly what you and Chiun are planning to do, but from hearing you talk, I think a lot of people could end up getting hurt."

"No one is going to get hurt," Chiun said.

"How can you be so sure—"

Chiun put his hand on the back of the boy's neck and said, "I am sure, and you can be sure, can't you, Walter?"

Walter's face went blank, and he nodded his head. "Yes."

"Good," Chiun said. He exerted a little more pressure, and suddenly Walter slumped over. Remo lowered him gently to the ground, where he began to snore.

"Put him in the alley behind the fence," Chiun said. "He will be out of the way there."

After Remo had taken care of Walter, he and Chiun prepared to cross the street. This time Remo himself stopped them.

"Do you see?"

"I see," Chiun said.

A man had come out the side door of the church,

carrying a black attaché case. He walked to a dark car, got in, and drove away.

"The drugs are on their way to the plant," Remo said. "By the time we get there, they should be in the fender wells of the cars."

"Let us go to church," Chiun said.

They crossed the street to the church and then moved around to the side entrance. Opening the door without a sound, they entered and stood out of sight behind Moorcock, who was already into his sermon.

"Sins of the flesh are not condemned here, my dear followers," he was saying, "as long as it is your own flesh you sin against. You may do what you will with your own body, your own mind, your own soul. *That* is a modern-day belief."

Remo and Chiun could see that the church was half-full. Most of the people were sitting toward the front, with the stragglers—winos and derelicts—toward the back.

Remo looked around and spotted a stairway leading up and a closed door near it. He nudged Chiun.

"Down," he said, pointing to the door.

They moved toward the door. Remo tried the knob, and it turned freely; he pushed the door open. The stairwell was dark, but at the bottom he could see a crack of light beneath another door. He led the way down, with Chiun right behind him. The stairs were wooden and rather flimsy, but he and Chiun barely touched them as they descended.

At the bottom Remo put his ear to the door and, listening intently, became aware of the sound of a man breathing on the other side. If he opened the door violently, the man was sure to turn and possibly sound an alarm. His best bet was to open the door normally and hope that the man simply thought it was Moorcock.

Remo opened the door and saw one man standing to his left. As he stepped through the door, the man began to turn slowly, opening his mouth to speak, but he never got the words out. Remo took him from behind, and with the touch of one hand, drove the life out of his body.

He lowered the man gently to the ground and looked around. There were about half a dozen other people in the basement, but none of them heard a thing, as they were busily performing their own tasks— mixing heroin with other white substances: salt, sugar, anything that closely resembled the drug. In its pure form, heroin was deadly to anyone who used it. The purer it was, however, the more times it could be "stepped on"—or "cut"—and the more times it was cut, the more it became worth on the street, because it could be stretched that much further. With the garbage junkies were used to shooting into their arms, this stuff would be like heaven.

It was interesting to Remo that the lighting in the basement was provided by kerosene lamps on the tables and the walls. Apparently Moorcock had seen no reason to fix the electricity in the basement. The basement was not finished, either. It was just concrete floors and bare walls, and Moorcock had moved wooden tables in where his people could do their jobs. If these people had had a union, they surely would have filed grievances about the working conditions.

Remo closed the door behind them and moved the body of the dead man aside.

"This is where they prepare the vile substance to be sold to children by children," Chiun said to Remo. "A doubly disgusting crime against the children of the world. These people must be punished in the severest manner."

"I agree, Chiun. Let's go."

They strode across the room to the half-dozen workers whose backs were to them. And they would have snuffed them out as effortlessly as so many candles, except that one of them chose to turn around at that moment. When he saw Remo and Chiun, he gaped and then shouted a warning to the others.

The others turned to face their imminent death, but one was quicker to think than the others. As he turned, he threw a handful of powder toward Remo. The grainy substance flew into Remo's eyes, burning and blinding him.

Remo backed up a step and gave full attention to his ears. He knew he would have to rely on his hearing to complete his task.

"They're both blind," someone yelled. "Get 'em."

Apparently Chiun was in a similar predicament, but Remo did not worry about the old man. Chiun could take care of himself. He closed his eyes tightly and listened intently.

The sound of three people rushing at him was deafening to his ultra-sensitive hearing, and the three were of such different sizes that he could easily discern one from the other.

The heaviest of the three reached him first. He

allowed the man to put his hands on him, then he reached out with his own hands, found the man's throat, and crushed it like an eggshell. The man croaked and gurgled as he slid to the floor and choked to death.

The other two reached him at the same time, each taking hold of one of his arms. He did not throw them both off because he would have had to locate them again in order to finish them off. Instead, he brought both of his arms around in front of him. With the men still hanging on to him, he kicked first one in the groin and then the other. They both screamed, and as they released his arms and fell to their knees, his hands shot out and took hold of their throats, ending their lives as he had the first man's.

That done, Remo listened for the sounds of Chiun's combat. He heard nothing.

"Chiun!"

"Here," Chiun replied. Following the sound of his master's voice, Remo also became aware of the sound of water. Chiun was washing out his eyes, a prospect that greatly appealed to Remo as well.

As Remo approached, Chiun reached out to take his hands and guide them into the water. Remo bathed his face and eyes several times until the burning subsided and his vision returned.

"We underestimated—" he started to say, flushing his eyes again, but Chiun didn't give him a chance to finish.

"I did not underestimate anyone, except perhaps you," the old man said. "I allowed the powder to enter my eyes so that I could set an example for you. That is all.''

Remo looked at Chiun, then nodded and said ''Of course, Little Father. You were an inspiration to me.''

''Of course,'' came the reply.

They both looked over at the dead men, and Remo saw that Chiun's three had met the same fate as his own.

''Well,'' he said, shaking the water from his hands, ''I guess the next step is to get those people upstairs out of here, and then take care of this place. These lamps ought to serve us nicely.''

''Yes,'' Chiun said, nodding, and then the old Oriental cocked his head as he heard something, ''Someone is coming.''

''I hear it,'' Remo said. Listening intently, he could hear noise in the stairwell, and he realized that there were two separate and distinct sets of footsteps.

They both turned to face the door as Lorenzo Moorcock entered the room, holding a terrified woman in front of him and pressing a gun to her right temple.

''Gentleman,'' Moorcock said, allowing the door to close behind them. ''Welcome to my little factory.''

''I guess we were pretty noisy, huh?'' Remo said. ''You came to complain?''

''On the contrary,'' Moorcock said. ''I'm here to compliment you. You've done my work for me.'' Moorcock looked at the bodies of his dead employees. ''Yes,'' he said, ''and very nicely too. You saved me the trouble of killing them myself.''

"Planning on pulling out?" Remo asked.

"Oh, yes, I believe the time has come for me to take my profits and move on," the minister said.

"Taking the lady with you?"

"Mrs. Sterling?" Moorcock said, tightening his arm around the woman's waist. "Oh, she insisted on coming down with me. The poor woman couldn't bear the thought of something happening to me."

"Please," the woman said at that point, her eyes pleading, "I don't understand."

"Be quiet," Moorcock said sharply. Looking at Remo and Chiun, Moorcock said, "We have a small emergency device set up down here that alerted me to your presence. I turned my congregation over to a guest speaker—a common practice—and asked Mrs. Sterling to accompany me. As you can see, she insisted on doing so."

Remo was feeling frustrated. He knew he could take Moorcock on without fear of his gun, but the gun wasn't pointing at him, it was pointing at Walter Sterling's mother.

Chiun was standing quietly, calmly staring at the minister. Remo knew that this was what Chiun had been waiting for, the opportunity to kill the man who had been responsible for the deaths of the children, and he knew that the Master of Sinanju must have been feeling some frustration of his own.

"What now, Moorcock?" Remo asked.

"Well, now you and your friend will join my people on the floor. Once I've gotten rid of you, I can return to my flock, wrap up my services, and be on my way."

"Where?"

Moorcock smiled and shook his head. "This is not the movies, sir, where the bad guy tells the good guys his entire plan because their death is imminent. If you're going to die, it would serve no purpose to tell you, save to postpone your deaths."

Still smiling, Moorcock aimed the gun at Remo and fired. When he saw that the bullet had missed, he acted quickly and snapped his arm back so that the gun was pressed against Mrs. Sterling's temple again.

"What trickery is this?" he demanded.

"Bad marksmanship?" Remo suggested.

"I am an excellent marksman," the minister said. "I couldn't have missed."

Remo shrugged and said, "You have to believe your own eyes, don't you?"

"There has to be another explanation," Moorcock said. "I can adapt to any situation." He was talking to himself as much as to Remo and Chiun.

"So I understand," Remo said. "You've adjusted to your failure in politics very nicely."

"You cannot anger me," Moorcock said. He stared at them for a few moments, then said, "I have it."

"Don't breathe this way; I haven't had my shots," Remo said.

"You," Moorcock said to Remo, ignoring the remark, "will kill him," pointing at Chiun, "or I shall kill her."

"That's a good plan," Remo said, "except for one thing."

"What's that?"

"If I try to kill him," Remo said, "I'm afraid that he'll kill me."

"That will serve my purpose just as well."

"Yeah, but if he kills me, who's going to kill him for you?" Remo asked.

"You are trying to confuse me in order to prolong your own life," Moorcock said. "You will kill the old man. That shouldn't be too much of a problem for you."

Remo could feel the scorn that remark brought out in his teacher.

"Please," he said to Moorcock, "don't get him mad."

"I think perhaps you are mad," Moorcock said. "This old man can hardly be a danger to anyone."

"If that's the way you feel," Remo said, "then you kill him."

All Remo or Chiun needed was for Moorcock to take the gun away from the woman's head once more, even for a few seconds. If the minister would fire at Chiun, then one of them would surely reach him before he could turn the gun back on Mrs. Sterling.

Moorcock was pondering the problem when something happened that resolved the situation. The basement door opened violently, striking Moorcock in the back. He staggered under the blow, releasing Mrs. Sterling so that she fell to the floor.

Moorcock himself retained his footing and turned to face the door. To everyone's surprise, Walter Sterling entered the room. When the boy saw the gun, he threw himself in front of his mother. Moorcock aimed the gun at him.

Chiun took full advantage of the situation, and
Remo stood back and watched because this was what
the Master of Sinanju had been waiting for. Remo
had done the legwork, but this part belonged to
Chiun.

The old Korean moved across the floor in a blur
and kicked the gun from Moorcock's hand. The minister shouted and turned to find himself face-to-face
with the old man he'd been ridiculing only moments
ago.

"I'll kill you," he said to Chiun.

"You have killed children," Chiun explained to
Moorcock, "and for that you must die a violent and
painful death."

Moorcock laughed and launched a punch at Chiun.
Chiun moved forward, easily avoiding the blow, and
landed a blow of his own. Remo was the only other
person in the room who heard the ribs on the man's
left side crack. Moorcock gasped but had no time to
slump to the floor before Chiun landed a second
blow, shattering the ribs on the right side. Remo
realized that Moorcock was about to suffer the Death
of a Thousand Breaks, which was usually reserved
for the very worst enemies of the House of Sinanju.

The sound of snapping bones filled the room, and
before long Moorcock was lying on the floor, barely
alive but still able to feel the pain from the damage
that had been inflicted on him by the Master of
Sinanju.

Chiun stepped back, surveyed his handiwork, and
nodded. Remo knew that there wasn't a whole bone
left in Moorcock's body.

"That was horrible," Mrs. Sterling said, sobbing. Her son had helped her to her feet, and she was leaning on him for support.

Chiun turned to the woman and said, "It was meant to be, madam."

Remo moved to Walter Sterling and put his hand on the boy's shoulder.

"What did he do to me?" Walter asked. "I woke up in an alley and—"

"Never mind," Remo said. "Walter, it's up to you and your mother to get all those people out of the building, and then you must call the police and tell them to come here."

"Should we wait—"

"After you've done that, take your mother home," Remo said. "We'll make sure that the police find evidence of what was going on here."

"All right," Walter said. He turned to his mother and told her they had to do what Remo said. Then he turned back to Remo and said, "The man who killed my father?"

"I'll take care of him, Walter," Remo said.

Walter Sterling accepted Remo's word and guided his mother up the steps.

Remo looked at Chiun, who was calmly studying the man on the floor. Moorcock was making all kinds of sounds, none of which sounded human.

Chiun looked at Remo then and said, "The lamps."

"Yes."

They waited several minutes for Walter to clean out the parishioners, then Remo took a few of the lamps from the walls and threw them onto the large wooden tables where the cutting had been done. The kerosene ignited the wood very quickly, and soon the acrid odor of burning heroin filled the air. Before long, everything that was wooden in the basement was burning, and Remo knew that it wouldn't be long before the flames found the steps and burned their way up to the main floor. The building was old, and it would go up quickly.

"Let's take him up," Remo said. He bent over and filled Moorcock's pockets with heroin, then threw the body over his shoulder and started up the steps.

When they reached the main level, they found that it was empty except for the smoke which had already begun to fill the place.

They left the church by the main exit. Remo left Moorcock there, where the police would be sure to find him.

There was a good chance that Lorenzo Moorcock would be dead by the time the police got there, but it could go either way.

"Next stop," Remo said, "National Motors."

Chiun looked at Moorcock, then nodded to Remo, and they went.

CHAPTER SIXTEEN

Jack Boffa and the man called Samuel, unaware of what was happening at the church, were busily tending to business at the National Motors plant.

First, Samuel turned the heroin over to Jack Boffa, all nicely cut and packed in plastic bags. Boffa had rounded up some of the kids to help him load the stuff in the fender wells of the cars that were being shipped that very day to New York, New Orleans, and Los Angeles. With both Louis Sterling and Allan Martin out of action, he needed the help.

Boffa, supervising the loading operation, was counting dollar signs in his head. He was to meet with Moorcock later that day—although he didn't know that the "big boss" was Moorcock—to collect his payment, unaware of the fact that Moorcock had intended to be gone long before their prearranged meeting. Even Samuel was to be left out in the cold—the cold ground, to be precise.

Both men worked diligently, unaware that they were working for no reason, unaware that they had dues to pay and that two men were on their way to collect.

In a big way.

When Remo and Chiun arrived at the plant, they presented themselves to the same receptionist Remo had dealt with earlier.

"Sweetheart, my father and I are going inside to conduct some business," Remo told her.

"Your . . . father?" she asked, staring at Chiun.

"Well, actually he's adopted," Remo said.

"He's adopted?"

"Yeah, you know. Send sixty-nine cents to support a child in an underprivileged country. Be a father and all that? Well, I chose to support an underprivileged adult and be a son. He came in the mail yesterday."

"In the mail?"

"Yeah. He would have been here sooner, but they sent him bulk rate."

"Oh—"

"Listen," Remo said, leaning across the desk and touching the girl behind the neck. She leaned into his touch with her eyes closed. "Would you do me a favor?"

"Anything."

"Why don't you take a coffee break. Go out, get yourself a cup of coffee and a doughnut—"

"I'm on a diet."

Damn, nobody stuck to a diet like a skinny woman, he thought.

"Have two cups of coffee, then," he said, "Black with no sugar. Drink them slowly, then find a pay phone and call the police. Tell them there's trouble at the plant and to come right away. And then you can take the rest of the day off and go home. Understand?"

"Yes," she said. "Whatever you say, but please . . ."

"What?"

She opened her eyes and said, "Would you come home with me?"

He smiled, removed his hand, and said, "Maybe later."

She sighed, collected her purse and jacket, waved at him, and left.

"Your father!" Chiun said in disgust.

"I was working on her resistance," Remo argued. "You know, lowering her defenses by making her feel sentimental."

"Wasting time," Chiun said.

"Come on, Chiun," Remo said. "You got your child killer. Lighten up."

"You are a constant source of embarrassment to me."

"You old sweet-talker, you. Come on, this way."

Remo led Chiun through the plant to the assembly line, where he was sure that the drug packing was well under way. As they reached that section, they opened the door a crack and peered in.

Remo saw Jack Boffa, still holding his clipboard, coordinating the operation, and saw that he had imported some of the kids to help out. He hoped Chiun wouldn't start in again, but that hope came too late.

"It continues," Chiun said when he saw what was going on.

"Chiun—"

"We must finish it."

"We will," Remo said. "That's what we're here for."

As they watched, a few cars came off the assembly line and were driven through a large garage-type door. Remo figured that the cars were being loaded onto one of those massive car-carrier trucks, to be transported to the three cities involved.

"Might as well get it done, Chiun," he said. He pushed the door open wide and walked in, with Chiun on his heels.

"Keep it moving there, boys," Jack Boffa was shouting. "We're almost through."

"Wrong, Boffa!" Remo shouted.

"Wha—" Boffa said, turning to face Remo. "Oh, you. Who's this, your houseboy?"

"Your operation is shut down, Boffa."

"What are you talking about?" the foreman demanded, trying to bluff it out. Remo was sure that the man did not have a gun on him, but he was aware that Louis Sterling had been killed with a knife.

"I mean the whole party is over. Your 'big boss' is in the hands of the police, and they're on their way here."

"I don't know what—"

"Hey, Mr. Boffa," a kid shouted. "A bag of shit opened. What should we—"

"Shut up!" Boffa shouted.

"You've got to learn to give up, Boffa," Remo advised him. "This is the end."

"No it ain't, dammit—" Boffa said, and out came the blade from behind the clipboard.

"Nasty," Remo said.

As Boffa slashed at him with the knife, Remo put out his bare hand. The blade collided with his flesh and snapped in two. The little demonstration shocked Boffa into silence.

"Bad steel," Remo said.

Boffa was staring at the broken blade when Remo took his clipboard away from him, which seemed to bother the man even more than having his knife broken.

"Hey, give me back my clipboard."

"You won't be needing it," Remo told him. "You're out of business—permanently."

Remo lashed out with the edge of the clipboard, catching Boffa on the side of the neck, and the man slumped to the floor in a lifeless heap.

"He who lives by the clipboard shall die by the clipboard," Remo said, dropping the clipboard on top of the body. He turned to Chiun and said, "The children are your responsibility, Chiun. Get them out of the way because I'm getting rid of that whole assembly line."

While Chiun herded the kids together like a bunch of lambs, Remo went to the head of the assembly line, where a gas pump stood. The cars were given just enough gas to be driven out to the car-carriers, but he took the hose and began to spray the passenger compartments of the vehicles.

Remo turned to make sure that Chiun had managed to get everybody outside before lighting a match and tossing it into the passenger compartment of the first car. The car ignited not with a bang but with a *whoosh*, and it occurred to Remo very briefly that perhaps he should have told the pretty young receptionist to call the fire department as well as the police department. He dismissed the thought as quickly as it arose, however. National Motors should have been more careful about who they hired and more observant about how their assembly line was being used—or misused.

Before long the second car ignited, and after a few moments the third, fourth, and fifth, in a domino effect.

Soon the entire assembly line was a mass of flames, and it was only because the gas tanks of the autos had not been filled that there were no explosions. Remo watched for a few minutes, and the air quickly filled with that odor again as the heroin went up in smoke.

Remo picked up the dead body of Jack Boffa, threw it over his shoulder and carried it out the way Chiun had taken the children. He hoped Chiun wouldn't come out of this whole thing with some kind of a Moses syndrome.

"Is that him?" Walter Sterling asked as Remo dropped the body to the ground.

He turned to face Walter, looking mildly surprised at the boy's arrival.

"Persistent, aren't you?"

"Is that the man who killed my father?"

"Yes, Walter, that's him."

Walter Sterling took one step forward and kicked Jack Boffa viciously on the side of the head.

"Kid, he's dead," Remo said, hoping he wasn't telling Walter anything that would upset him greatly. "He didn't feel a thing."

"That's okay," the kid said, "I did."

Remo turned to face a couple of those massive car carriers and said to Chiun, "Ask the kids if those cars are loaded down with drugs."

"They are."

"Well, then, they have to go too," Remo said. "And they're going to go big, Chiun, so take the kids out front to meet the cops. They ought to be here soon. When I come out, I'll be bringing Boffa with me, with his broken knife. The cops'll find traces of blood on it. Oh, and get me a bag of heroin, and then have the kids throw the rest of the stuff into those cars before they go."

"Anything else?" Chiun asked, with a sarcastic bow.

"Let's just get this over with."

Chiun seemed to agree with that and went off to talk to his flock. There were about a dozen kids of fifteen and sixteen. They filed over to the carriers and started dumping the remainder of their supply into the open windows of the cars. Chiun brought Remo a nickel bag and then again herded the kids away from the area. Remo bent over and stuffed the bag into the pocket of the dead foreman. Then he said, "Get lost, Walter. These cars have some gas in the tanks, and they may blow."

"Can't I help?"

"Do you have any matches?"

"Yes."

"Okay, I'll use your matches."

Walter took out a box of stick matches, handed them to Remo, and then went off in the direction that Chiun had taken the others.

Remo searched the area and came up with some rags, which he soaked with gasoline. He undid the gas cap on one car from each carrier, stuffed his makeshift fuses in, and then lit them and backed away a respectable distance.

He was aware of sirens in the distance just as the first car blew. Again, the domino effect came into play as car after car on the first carrier also burst into flames. By the time the police arrived, both carriers were a mass of flames, and now, of course, there was the danger that the full gas tanks of the carriers would explode.

Well, Remo thought, you can't make an omelet without breaking a few eggs.

"I'm wondering," Detective William Palmer said to Remo and Chiun, "why I always manage to be one step behind you."

"We sent people to call in," Remo said. "Maybe they stopped for coffee on the way."

"Yeah," Palmer said, "maybe."

"Besides, what's the difference?" Remo said. He looked over to where some uniformed police were handcuffing all of the kids under the watchful eye of Chiun. "You've just about got the whole thing wrapped up now."

"So you say," Palmer said. "I've got a fire in a church and a fire here at the plant. Luckily, the fire trucks got here before the gas tanks on those carriers blew, or the whole plant would be gone."

"Omelets and eggs," Remo muttered.

"What was that?"

"Nothing."

"I've got a dead preacher with his pockets full of smack, and I've got a dead foreman with *his* pockets full of smack. I wonder who put it there?"

"They did?" Remo sugggested.

"They aren't saying," Palmer said pointedly.

"Well, I wish I could help you, Detective," Remo said, "but every time we showed up, it was just a little bit late. We sent word to you as soon as we could."

"I'd like to believe that, but I'm afraid you and your friend are going to have to come with me and answer some questions. My ass could be in a sling because of this."

"I don't think so."

"Oh, and why don't you think so?"

"Well, you've got the whole story in your hands," Remo said. "All you've got to do is ask those kids."

"Those kids?" Williams asked. "Those kids all have rap sheets as long as your arm, mister."

"All juvenile stuff, right?"

"So?"

"You talk to Walter Sterling," Remo said. "He'll

give you the straight story, and then let him talk to those other boys.''

"You know, I don't know who you are, and I don't know why I keep sticking my neck out for you. . . .''

"It's the little boy in me," Remo said. "The little boy.''

CHAPTER SEVENTEEN

When Remo showed up at Folcroft, he was alone.

"Where's Chiun?" Smith asked.

"Oh, he said he had something to attend to," Remo hedged.

"Well, I guess I don't need to hear the whole story from both of you. Is it wrapped up?"

"With a pretty bow," Remo said. "Moorcock cooked up the whole scam after he saw how his minister bit was going over. He was pulling in a lot of money and decided to put it to work for him. His Iranian contacts didn't hurt, either."

"Well, I'm sure the Iranians weren't helping him out of the goodness of their hearts," Smith said. "They must have seen this as a means to undermine the youth of the United States."

That was exactly what Chiun had said before he went off on his private little quest, Remo thought, only Chiun hadn't said "undermine." He had said "destroy."

181

"Well, anyway," Remo continued, "it all started to fall apart when some of the kids working for him started to get an attack of conscience. If it wasn't the kids, it was the parents, like in the Martin case."

"So people started getting out of line, Moorcock started getting rid of them, and we noticed."

"Right," Remo said. "The beginning of the end."

"Fortunately for us," Smith said.

"All of the kids we turned over to the cops in Detroit started talking right after Walter Sterling did," Remo explained, "so the police pretty much have a picture of what went on. What they don't know, they can pretty well reconstruct."

"And you're out of it?"

"We got lucky with that cop, Palmer," Remo said. "He recognized something good and noble in me."

"You don't say."

"He was also working the case from a different angle, as it turns out," Remo said.

"What angle was that?"

"Moorcock had paid the judge who set the bail for the Martin kid."

"But the judge set the bail exorbitantly high."

"Right, and who would suspect the minister of a half-assed church of putting up the money? That was just a little extra insurance to make sure nothing got back to him."

"He was pretty thorough, wasn't he, this minister?" Smith said.

"Not thorough enough," Remo said.

*   *   *

In a Mexico City hotel room, Rafael Cintron was waiting with his two colleagues, Antonio Jiminez and Pablo Santoro, for some Iranian diplomats to arrive for a conference.

"It is unfortunate what happened to Señor Moorcock in Detroit," he said to the other two, "but we are fortunate that the Iranians wish to seek another avenue in order to keep our, er, business flourishing. After all, they paid us quite a lot of money to carry their drugs during our trips to the United States and are willing to continue to do so."

"We are with you, Rafael," Jiminez said. "You have no need to convince us."

Cintron looked at the other man, Santoro, who nodded his agreement. "Excellent," he said. He had gotten used to the life-style he had been enjoying on the money the Iranians paid him and was very happy that he would not have to choose between his wife and his mistress but could continue to support both.

When the knock finally sounded at the door, he jumped up from his seat and said, "At last!" The others watched as he walked eagerly to the door and swung it open.

"Welcome, my friend—" Cintron started to say, but as the man in the doorway started to fall forward, Cintron was forced to leap out of the way. "What . . ." he said, and they all gaped at the fallen man, who was obviously dead.

"Watch out!" Jiminez shouted, and Cintron turned to see that there had been another man right behind the first, and now he was falling forward too. Cintron jumped out of the way in time to avoid the second man, then did a dance step to avoid being hit by a third.

"*Dios mio*," Cintron said, staring down at the three dead men. From what he could see, there wasn't a mark on any of them, but they were quite dead.

"How—" Santoro asked.

"I don't know."

"I do," a small, elderly Oriental said, stepping into the room through the open door.

All three men looked at him in disbelief.

"Who—who are you?" Cintron asked.

"I am a man who is concerned about the health of the youth of the United States."

"What?"

"These men were trying to destroy it," the Oriental gentleman went on, "and you men were helping them. You see the price they paid, so you can guess the price you must pay."

"You're mad," Cintron said.

"You killed them?" Jiminez asked, knowing that the question was ridiculous.

"Oh, yes," the Oriental said.

"That's preposterous," Cintron said. "How could you have—"

"Easily," the man said. "I am acting on behalf of the children of America and of the world. I am their instrument."

"He is *loco*," Santoro said.

"We must leave," Cintron said. "Something is very wrong."

"*Si*, we must leave," Jiminez agreed.

They gathered up their belongings and turned to

leave but found the way blocked by the elderly Oriental, who looked frail enough to be knocked over by a stiff breeze—until you looked at his eyes.

His eyes were frightening.

"Let us pass."

"I will let you pass . . . on," the man said, and started toward them.

Cintron did not exactly see what the old Oriental did, but suddenly Jiminez slumped to the floor, just as dead as the three Iranians, and without a mark on him.

"What happened?" Cintron asked, looking at Santoro, but by that time Santoro had also slumped to the floor, dead. "This is insane," he said.

"Yes," Chiun said, before he killed Rafael Cintron, "that is just what the destruction of children is. Insane."

"So when do you expect Chiun back?" Smith asked.

"He won't be long," Remo said. "He's just making sure that the children of the world are safe. He's a very concerned citizen, you know."

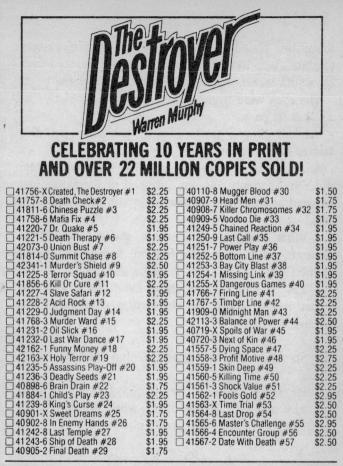